William Forsyth

Rome and its Ruins

William Forsyth

Rome and its Ruins

ISBN/EAN: 9783337382025

Printed in Europe, USA, Canada, Australia, Japan

Cover: Foto ©Andreas Hilbeck / pixelio.de

More available books at **www.hansebooks.com**

ROME AND ITS RUINS.

WILLIAM FORSYTH, M.A. Q.C. M.P.

Late Fellow of Trinity College, Cambridge.

AUTHOR OF "HORTENSIUS;" "HISTORY OF TRIAL BY JURY;" "THE LIFE
OF CICERO," ETC.

With Map and numerous Illustrations.

PUBLISHED UNDER THE DIRECTION OF
THE COMMITTEE OF GENERAL LITERATURE AND EDUCATION,
APPOINTED BY THE SOCIETY FOR PROMOTING
CHRISTIAN KNOWLEDGE.

———

SOCIETY FOR PROMOTING CHRISTIAN KNOWLEDGE;
SOLD AT THE DEPOSITORIES :
77, GREAT QUEEN STREET, LINCOLN'S INN FIELDS;
4, ROYAL EXCHANGE; 48, PICCADILLY ;
AND BY ALL BOOKSELLERS.

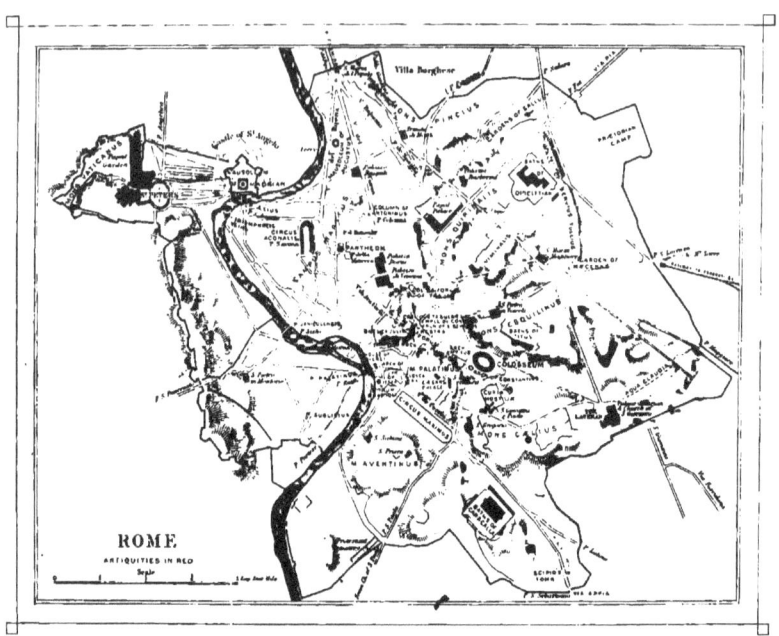

ROME

ANTIQUITIES IN RED

ROME AND ITS RUINS.

Rome Pagan and Rome Papal! How much is
contained in these four words! How we are carried back to the days of our early youth, when
painfully at school we were taught the early
history of Rome! We see Æneas and his companions, the wandering fugitives from Troy, landing at the mouth of the Tiber,—which was then,
as Virgil describes it, but is now no longer,
shaded by leafy groves,—and sending a peaceful
embassy to King Latinus. Afterwards, when war
broke out between the Trojans and the Latins, we
see Æneas himself sailing up the Tiber to solicit
the friendship and aid of Evander, the aged
Arcadian king, whose city of Palantium was in
the low ground beneath the Palatine Hill. We see
the furious contest raging between the strangers
and the inhabitants of Latium, in which Turnus,
the king of the Rutulians, on the one side, and
Æneas on the other, fought for the hand of

Lavinia. We see the infant city of Romulus traced out by a ploughshare ; and Remus, his twin brother—who, like him, had been suckled by the she-wolf—struck down and killed, because in contempt he leaped over the rising wall, and dared thus to insult the future majesty of Rome. These are, indeed, but fables ; but they are fables so interwoven in our memories that no cold historical criticism will ever be able to efface them ; and, even now, when we wander on the Aventine Hill we half expect to discover the cave of that famous old robber, Cacus, the son of Vulcan, and lineal ancestor of the Highland caterans, whose career was cut short by Hercules, who strangled him for stealing his cattle,—a feat which he had accomplished by dragging them backwards by their tails into his den.

But it is not my purpose here to dwell on the history of the past; and we must confine our attention to the city as it exists at the present day.

First, however, we must get to Rome, and to do this we have the choice of several routes. The shortest and most expeditious and least fatiguing journey is to go from Paris to Marseilles, and there embark on board the French steamer—an extremely good one—which sails direct to Civita

Vecchia. It performs the voyage in about thirty-eight hours, so that the whole distance from London to Rome may be easily accomplished in four days. Another route is this: You go from

CIVITA VECCHIA.

Marseilles to Nice by land, having the advantage of the railway as far as Cannes, and from Nice by the beautiful Corniche Road, between the foot of the Maritime Alps and the Mediterranean, as

far as Genoa, from which place there is a steamer
to Leghorn and Civita Vecchia. Or you may, if
you prefer it, avoid Marseilles altogether, and go
from Paris by railway to Chambéry, and thence
cross the Mont Cenis to Turin, from which place
there is a railway direct to Genoa. I have tried
all these routes, and I think I give the preference
to that by way of Nice and the Corniche Road.

Let us, however, suppose that we have reached
Civita Vecchia by a steamer, either from Genoa or
Marseilles,—and before we land you may observe
the navy of the Pope, consisting of a single steam-
boat lately built for him in England, at anchor in
the harbour. I must do the Pope the justice to
say that the arrangements made for landing and
embarking at Civita Vecchia, the only port on the
Mediterranean—as Ancona *was* on the Adriatic
—side of the Papal States, are admirable. Formerly it was notorious for extortion and dis-
comfort, and the unhappy traveller was the prey
of a host of harpies who exist in Italy under the
name of *facchini*, of which the translation, as
given in the dictionaries, is " porters" and " scoun-
drels," and who seize upon your luggage and treat
you very much as a keeper would a maniac.
Nothing of the kind, however, is now allowed at

Civita Vecchia. There is a fixed and moderate tariff of charges—one franc for landing in a boat at the pier, and another franc for the carriage of luggage, no matter how large, to the omnibus which conveys it to the railway. It is a great and useful reform, to be lauded by all travellers; and I can only say of it, with reference to the general government of the Papal States, *O si sic omnia !*

The distance from Civita Vecchia to Rome by the railway is forty-two miles, but it took me two hours and a half to accomplish it. On leaving the town, we enter at once upon the Campagna—that immense plain which spreads on every side around Rome like a sea of desolation. Not that it is all a level plain: in many places it is a succession of low swelling downs with deep ravines, and here and there they rise to the dignity of small hills ; but at a distance, or seen from the top of any lofty building in Rome, it looks, as a friend with whom I travelled remarked, just like Romney Marsh— a barren and deserted waste. It is not, however, altogether barren, for portions are cultivated ; and I saw, in several places, large grey oxen, with huge horns like those of buffaloes, ploughing the soil. But the Campagna is notoriously unhealthy, and one of the most curious of physical problems is to discover the cause of this. In old times it was very different. Then—I speak of the times anterior to the foundation of Rome, and also long after that period—it swarmed with a busy population. Cities, of some of which the very site is now a matter

THE CAMPAGNA.

of controversy, were then built and inhabited, such as Fidenæ and Antemnæ and Gabii and Collatia and Veii and Crustumerium and Ardea, and many others. But towards the end of the Republic, if not before, it was considered, in parts at all events, as pestilential; and the *malaria*, the curse that broods over it, was as well known to the ancient as to the modern Romans.

Now what is the cause of this unhealthiness? The theories on the subject are various, but the most satisfactory seems to be that adopted by Dr. Arnold, in his History of Rome, who attributes it to the want of moisture, and says,* "If, then, more rain fell in the Campagna formerly than is the case now; if the streams were full of water, and their course more rapid; above all, if owing to the uncleared state of Central Europe, and the greater abundance of wood in Italy itself, the summer heats set in later, and were less intense, and more often reduced by violent storms of rain, there is every reason to believe that the Campagna must have been far healthier than at present; and that formerly, in proportion to the clearing and cultivation of Central Europe, to the felling of the woods in Italy itself, the consequent decrease in the quantity of rain, the shrinking of the streams, and the disappearance of the water of the surface, has been the increased unhealthiness of the country and the more extended range of the malaria."

To this, however, must be added the fact of the absence of animal life in later times, except to an

* History of Rome, i. 505.

inconsiderable extent, and of fires, both which circumstances have no doubt contributed greatly to the unhealthiness of the district.*

As we get our first sight of the Tiber, close beside which during part of the latter half of our journey the railway runs, we see at once why it was called *Flavus Tiberis*, or the "Yellow Tiber"—

* There is a curious confirmation of this in the account given of some parts of India by Count de Warren in his work, "L'Inde Anglaise in 1843," vol. iii. p. 63 :—

"Des lieux célebrès de l'Inde autrefois pour la pureté de l'air et la salubrité du climat, exhalent aujourd'hui des miasmes pestilentiels et sont litteralement inhabitables ; on disait que comme au temps de Sodome et de Gomorrhe, la terre s'ouvre pour laisser échapper des gaz qui devorent la population. Tel à été le sort de Ghouty, tel sera celui de Bellary. Ce qui est encore plus extraordinaire, c'est que ce changement a eu lieu généralement en raison inverse des causes qui auraient dû purifier ces localités ; il a suivi la substitution de la propreté et de la ventilation d'un cantonnement Européen à l'entassement et à la saleté de la population native. Ainsi, tant que les forts de Ghouty, Nundidroog, Guigi, Seringapatam, presentaient chacun une fourmilière humaine entassée dans des huttes fétides, le choléra et les fièvres typhoids étaient des maladies inconnues. On ne trouve aujourd'hui dans ces mêmes lieux que des casernes abandonnées et en ruines ; tout y est d'une propreté exquise, et cependant une seule nuit passée dans une de ces casernes est généralement suffisante pour développer le germe d'une maladie sinon mortelle au moins destructive du tempérament. Observons encore que trois d'entre elles sont sur des montagnes à une grande élévation au dessus des plaines environnantes, eloignées de tout marécage, et presque absolument privées d'eau."

although I think that "muddy yellow" would be a more appropriate epithet—for the colour is very much like that of water in a marl-pit, especially after any considerable quantity of rain. Its average breadth seems to be about two thirds of

THE TIBER.

that of the Thames at Westminster Bridge; but in some places it is wider, as, for instance, where it flows on each side of the island in Rome called *Isola di Roma*, which reminds one of the island in the Seine at Paris on which stands the Cathedral of Notre Dame, and the whole of the city originally stood.

The view of Rome as we approach the city is very much interfered with, and, in fact, partly hidden, by an elevated ridge in front to the left. This is the Janiculum Hill, and behind it, to the east, are St. Peter's and the Vatican. But in the distance on the right we see a long line of broken arches stretching south along the Campagna like the leg of a gigantic spider. These are the ruins of the famous aqueduct constructed by the Emperor

AQUEDUCT.

Claudius to supply Rome with water. For it is

said that the Romans were ignorant of the hydro-static law that water confined in a tube rises to the level of its source, and they therefore went to the enormous expense of building an open aque-duct to convey water from the Alban hills to the city. Between these arches and the railway there is another dark line of dotted ruins, not continuous, like the aqueduct, and low in height—all except one. Those ruins are the tombs of the Appian Way, and that one is the tomb of Cæcilia Metella, of which we shall say more by and by. Beyond all these, on the right, that is, towards the east, is the glorious range of the Latin Hills.

The railway-station is about half a mile from the walls, and you have to traverse an uninterest-ing suburb before you enter the gate and find yourself actually in Rome. I entered by the Porta S. Pancraza, but there is one nearer the station called Porta Portese, through which the road leads across the island of the Tiber to the left bank on the other side where the city stands.

It is seldom safe to judge by a first impression, and I must candidly confess that my first impres-sions on entering the city were those of disappoint-ment. The streets seemed mean and common-place; and, except the majestic dome of St. Peter's

on my left, I looked in vain for anything to indicate that I was in the Eternal City, until I passed
the Column of Antonine in the Piazza Colonna,
which opens into the Corso. But I soon found
that I was wrong; and every day I spent in Rome
made me feel more and more that I was on classic
ground, and increased the interest I felt in everything around me. Those dull streets through
which I had passed in an omnibus were part of
the Campus Martius, once a verdant plain outside
the ancient wall, interspersed with noble monuments, where the Roman generals, who demanded
a triumph, remained with their armies, not being
allowed to enter the city until the Senate had
passed their decree respecting it. The Campus
Martius was originally the domain land of the
Tarquins; and when Tarquinius Superbus was
expelled from Rome it was confiscated, and dedicated to Mars as a public park. Hence the name.
Gibbon says,* "Amidst his other great designs
for embellishing the city, Augustus did not forget
the Campus Martius. He adorned it with beautiful buildings, and arranged for the grandees of
Rome to follow his example. None imitated him
more eagerly than his son-in-law Agrippa, of

* Miscellaneous Works, p. 482.

whose magnificence the septa, baths, gardens, lake or basin, and above all the Pantheon, were conspicuous proof. In the time of Strabo the suburb of the Campus Martius was but little inferior to the city itself. Its populousness, however, was never proportional to its extent; the public garden occupied much ground, and there was still an empty space for the military exercise of the Roman youth." The bulk of the modern city now stands on this site, and modern Rome may be said to be comprised between the Pincian Hill and the Tiber, that girdles the western side of the Campus Martius. The Corso, a long straight street, which is one of the main arteries of Rome, occupies the ground of the Via Lata, or Broadway, which ran between the Porta Flaminia (now the Porta del Popolo) on the north, and the Porta Ratumena on the south in the old wall of Servius Tullius at the foot of the Capitol.

I had often heard that, owing to the changes that had taken place in the conformation of the ground, and the accumulation of rubbish during the lapse of ages, it was now difficult to make out the Seven Hills; but this is a mistake. They are distinctly visible if care is taken to select the proper point of view; but the traveller who goes to

Rome under the idea that these hills ever were of a considerable height will be disappointed. The Romans, with perhaps pardonable pride, called them *montes*, but they had no more dignified term

THE SEVEN HILLS.

to apply to the Alps themselves. They had a word (*colles*) for hills as distinguished from mountains; but it is very seldom used by the Latin writers when speaking of the hills of Rome. The three most conspicuous, and of which the features are the most plainly marked, are the Aventine, the Palatine, and the Capitoline; next to these I

would place in order the Cœlian, the Quirinal, and
the Esquiline ; and last the Viminal, which is low
and flat, and by no means easy to discover. Indeed
without the aid of a guide book and local information I could never feel sure that the Viminal was
a hill at all ; and it is not certain that it *was* one
of the Seven Hills, and not rather merely a part or
adjunct of the Esquiline. But we must disabuse
our minds of any exaggerated idea as to the size
and height of any of these famous hills. Some of
them, such as the Cœlian, the Viminal, and the
Esquiline, are rather what we should call rising
grounds than hills. I rode one day to the Mons
Sacer, about three miles from Rome to the north-
east, famous as the place to which the Plebs retired in the year 493 B.C. when—their patience
having been utterly exhausted by the oppressive
tyranny of the Patricians, into whose power most
of them had fallen as debtors, according to the
terribly severe law of debtor and creditor at Rome
—they determined not to return to the city until
they obtained some guarantee for their rights
and liberties. It was then, according to the
account given by Livy, that Menenius Agrippa
induced them to come back by relating to
them the well-known fable of the belly and the

members; but in reality the sedition was appeased
by the concession on the part of the Patricians
that magistrates called Tribunes, armed with
immense powers, should be created, to defend the
interests of the Plebeians. I found this celebrated *Mons* or hill to be a mere swelling on the
right bank of the Anio—up which it was easy to
canter. The most abrupt of the seven hills are
the Aventine, the Palatine, and the Capitoline;
and of these the two former are the least changed
in shape,. and are most like what they were in
appearance when Rome was first founded. There
is no hill to compare with the Castle Rock at
Edinburgh. The Palatine is not so high as the
Carlton Hill there, and Clifton rises above Bristol
to a greater elevation than any of the seven hills
above the level of Rome. I once went up to the
top of St. Peter's and stood in the ball there, from
which the view is most magnificent. But as I
ascended, and long before I reached even the dome,
all appearance of the hills which lie to the south-
east of the cathedral had vanished.

The best place to take your stand in order to
get a good idea of Rome is the Tower of the
Capitol; and I propose that we should go there
together, and I will point out the principal features

of the view, and say a few words on the different objects in the panorama around us.

But first let me try and give some idea of the Capitol itself.

It consists of a saddle-backed ridge running east and west, of which the side to the west, known by the name of Monte Caprino, on which stands the Palazzo Caffarelli, is the highest. That to the east is crowned by the curious old Church of Ara Cœli, and between these two more elevated portions of the hill is a depression, called by some authors the Intermontium,* where the Palace of the Senator now stands, with the tower in the centre, on which we are supposed to have taken up our position. In order to reach the Capitol from the north or city side we enter an open square called the Piazza d'Ara Cœli, from which a flight of steps ascends to a small courtyard or square called Piazza di Campidoglio (the modern name for the Capitol), with the Palace of the Senator opposite in our front, and two wings on each side. The Campidoglio, or " Field of Pain," was so called from its being used in the middle ages as the place for the execution of criminals; and the word "Capitol" has been

* It was here that Romulus placed his *Asylum*, a place of refuge for outlaws.

derived (though it is hardly necessary to remark that this is a fabulous etymology suggested by the name) from Caput Toli, "the head of Tolus;" because in digging the foundations of the Temple of Jupiter there, in the reign of one of the Tarquins, a bleeding head was discovered, which was said to have been the head of a man named Tolus. The wing on the right in the Palace of the Conservators contains a gallery of pictures, the Bronze Wolf, and many

THE BRONZE WOLF.

curious antiquities; and the one on the left hand, called the Museum of the Capitol, is appropriated to ancient sculpture. Here we find, among other celebrated statues, the Dying Gladiator, the Antinous, and the Capitoline Venus. The Palace of the Senator and both the wings of the courtyard

were built from the designs of Michael Angelo;
but I confess their appearance greatly disappointed me, and they are hardly worthy of occupying so famous a spot, which was in old times
pre-eminently distinguished by the sumptuous
magnificence of its buildings. At the top of the
steps which lead up to the court or piazza, which
is faced on the north side by a balustrade, are two
colossal statues in marble of Castor and Pollux,
each standing by the side of a horse; and in
the centre of the court is the noble equestrian
statue of the Emperor Marcus Aurelius. Both
the horse and the rider are of bronze, which was
originally gilt, and Michael Angelo was so struck
with the action of the horse, which looks as if it
would prance off the pedestal on which it stands,
that as he gazed upon it he exclaimed, " *Cammina!* "
" It walks! " I ought to have mentioned that
before ascending the stairs we observe on our left
hand a long flight of marble steps leading up to
the Church of Ara Cœli, or Altar of Heaven, with
its unfinished *façade* of plain and unadorned brick
like the front of a huge barn. It is generally
supposed to occupy the site of the Temple of
Jupiter Capitolinus, and it was in this church that
Gibbon first conceived the idea of writing the

" Decline and Fall of the Roman Empire." It would
be difficult to imagine a more appropriate spot.
He says that it was on the 15th October, 1764, as
he sat there musing amidst the ruins of the
Capitol, while the bare-footed friars were singing
vespers, that the idea of writing the work first
occurred to his mind.

The Palace of the Senator is so called because
it is the official residence of the Senator—the
head of the municipal body at Rome.   I met him
one day in his state equipage, which reminded
me very much of the Lord Mayor's carriage.   The
palace rests upon the substruction of a very ancient
building, the *Tabularium*, in which the archives
of the State were kept when Rome was yet a
republic.   From an inscription which has been
found there, it appears that the *Tabularium* of
which the remains now exist (for possibly there
was a still older building on the same site) was
built by Lutatius Catulus, about eighty years
before Christ.   It formed a kind of face to the
south side of the Capitol, rising up from the
northern extremity of the Forum, with which it
communicated by a large door or gate and a flight
of steps leading down from it to the Forum.
There is a very interesting account in Tacitus

of an attack made on the Capitol by the soldiers
of the Emperor Vitellius when it was occupied by
the partisans of Vespasian, his rival for the throne ;
and in the conflict the Temple of Jupiter Capitolinus was set on fire, and with the adjacent
buildings destroyed. Tacitus mentions that when
the door of the Capitol (by which I suppose him
to mean the door of the Temple) was burnt, the
entrance was barricaded by statues which were
pulled down from their pedestals for the purpose,
and so the assailants were prevented from rushing
in at that part ; but they climbed up in two other
places, one by the Tarpeian Rock, and the other
near what he calls the *Lucus Asyli,* and made
themselves masters of the Capitol.

But where *was* the Temple of Jupiter Capitolinus ? Was it on the eastern or western
summit of the Capitoline ridge ? In other words,
was it on the site of the modern church of Ara
Cœli, or was it where the Palazzo Caffarelli stands
on the Monte Caprino ? Upon the correct deter-
mination of this spot depends many a topo-
graphical problem at Rome. The space between
the two heights which, following later authorities,
I have called the *Intermontium,* was known by that
name to the ancients. Those two heights (the

Ara Cœli and the Monte Caprino) were originally, covered with wood, and they are spoken of as "the two groves"—one of which seems afterwards to have been the Ara Cœli, and the other the Capitolium, properly so called. The intermediate space was the Asylum Romuli. Thus Strabo says Romulus established an "*asylum*" between the Ara and the Capitolium. Livy (i. 8) speaks of it as a place between the two groves. Dionysius (ii. 27) says, "the space between the Capitol and the Ara is now called by the Romans 'between the two groves.'" Bunsen, after reviewing the conflicting authorities, decides against the Ara Cœli, and in favour of the Monte Caprino, or western height, as the site of the Temple of Jupiter, and he places the Temple of Juno Moneta where the Church of Ara Cœli now stands. The Ara, according to him, embraced more than any one particular point, and included the eastern summit. He therefore exactly reverses the positions which have been usually assumed. It seems certain that the words Ara and Capitolium were loosely used by the ancient writers sometimes to designate particular parts of the hill, and sometimes the whole of it. Hence much confusion arises, and it is difficult to reconcile apparently conflicting passages. The celebrated antiquary Canina, whose opinion is entitled to great weight, has no hesitation in placing the Temple of Jupiter on the Ara Cœli, and he says that discoveries have been made there which seem to place the matter beyond a doubt. There is, however, a good deal of difficulty in understanding the exact positions of the buildings to which Tacitus refers. It would, I think, be removed by supposing that the Temple of Jupiter stood over the Tabularium, but I know of no authority to support this view. Tacitus (Hist. iii. 71), in describing the attack which caused the conflagration, says that the Vespasian party who defended the Capitol against the Vitellians mounted the hill as far as the first door of the *arx* of the Capitol. Now the *arx* was on the west side of the *Intermontium*, just above the Tarpeian Rock, and at a considerable distance from the Temple of Jupiter on the east. He then says that some porticoes on the right hand of the *Clivus Capitolinus* as you ascend were set on fire, and the Vitellians followed the course of the flames, and would have forced their way through the burnt doors of the Capitol if Sabinus had not barricaded the entrance with some statues which were pulled down for the purpose. Afterwards, he says, the flames caught

the wooden figures of some eagles, which supported
the roof, but he does not explain of what building;
and he immediately adds, "Thus the Capitol, with
its doors closed, and neither defended nor plundered, became a prey to the conflagration." He
then goes on to mourn over this destruction of
the *Capitolium*, of which he says the foundations
had been laid by Tarquinius Priscus, in consequence of a vow in the Sabine war, and which
Servius Tullius and Tarquinius Superbus had
afterwards completed out of spoils taken from
the enemy, but Horatius Pulvillus, when Consul
for the second time, had consecrated. He therefore
clearly uses the word Capitolium to signify the
Temple. If so, the "burnt doors of the Capitol"
cannot be the same as the "doors of the *arx* of
the Capitol;" and if the Temple occupied the site
of the Church of Ara Cœli, as is always assumed,
the fire must have mounted up from the porticoes
to the building above them, and so spread east-
ward to the Temple. The truth is, that the word
Capitolium is used loosely by the Latin writers
in different senses. Sometimes it designates the
whole of the buildings on the hill, sometimes the
Ara, on the western summit, sometimes the Tem-
plum, on the eastern. I may add that we learn

from the interesting account which Tacitus gives
us (Hist. iv. 53), of the laying of the foundations
of the new temple to replace that which had been
burnt down, that it was dedicated not to Jupiter
alone, but to Jupiter, Juno, and Minerva.

The door leading to the Tabularium from the
Forum was afterwards walled up, and the Temple
of Vespasian was erected in front of it, where
the stairs connecting it with the Forum formerly
stood.

The lower part of the Tabularium has only
within the last twenty years been excavated and explored. It was built of massive masonry, consisting
of enormous blocks of the kind of stone which is
called *tufa*, a volcanic formation; and as I was
asked by the guide to apply my tongue to the
fragment, and found it was decidedly saltish, I at
first fancied that the stone was some sort of saline
deposit, until he informed me that part of the
ancient corridor where we were standing had been
used in the middle of the fifteenth century as a
magazine of salt, which, if true, may perhaps
account for the taste of the stone. I need not
give a description of the plan of the building,
with its subterranean chambers, and galleries, and
stairs. It will be enough to say that no one can

fail to be struck with the vast size and strength
of the walls, and the rude magnificence of the
interior.

I have mentioned the Tarpeian Rock ; and, as it
is in the immediate neighbourhood of the spot
where I suppose ourselves to be placed—that is,
on the tower of the Capitol, and facing south—I
will endeavour to point it out.   But this is not so
easy as might be imagined.   Everybody knows
that it was the place where criminals were hurled
down in the stern old times of Republican Rome,
but the exact spot is matter of controversy, and
two places claim the honour of what we can
hardly call the Lover's Leap.   The one is behind
us, on the north-west side of the Capitol, where
there is a villanously dirty little street—a *cul de
sac*—full of unutterable abominations, and called
Vicolo della Rupe Tarpeia.   I came upon it ac-
cidentally one day with a friend, and we ventured
to pick our steps up for a few yards until we
reached a precipitous face of rock, which, supposing the mass of houses and accumulated
deposit below to be cleared away, would seem
very well fit for the purpose of breaking one's
neck by a fall ; and therefore, so far as height and
steepness were necessary for that object, this might

have been the Tarpeian Rock, as it professes to be. But it cannot have been the real place of execution, for we know that that fronted the Forum, which is on the other—that is, the south—side of the Capitol. We learn this fact from many passages

TARPEIAN ROCK.

in the Latin writers, but especially from what Dionysius tells us, in relating the account of the execution of Spurius Cassius, namely, that he was taken to the precipice that overhangs the Forum, and in the presence of the multitude thrown down the rock; "for this," he adds, "was then the usual capital punishment with the Romans." And he says in effect the same when speaking of the proceedings against Coriolanus. When the

Gauls had captured Rome, and a band of these barbarians was climbing up to the Capitol by night, M. Manlius Capitolinus was awakened by the cackling of some geese, which were kept in the Temple of Juno; and, having given the alarm, hurled down the assailants, and so saved the Capitol. The French now occupy Rome; and not long ago there appeared a caricature representing a French soldier on the Capitol plucking the feathers of a goose, with the words beneath, "A Gaul's revenge."* There can be no doubt, therefore, that we must look for this famous rock on the south or Forum side of the Capitol; and a place is shown at the edge of some gardens on the Monte Caprino, to the west of the tower of the Capitol, which is called, and very probably is, the real Tarpeian Rock. Wherever it was, Tacitus mentions that in his time it was approached by a flight of a hundred steps,† all trace of which has entirely disappeared; but very probably, if proper

---

* This story is told in Ampère's *L'Histoire Romaine a Rome*, a very instructive and amusing work. The following epigram, which I wrote, may serve to express the same senti-ment:—

"A Gallis anser Romam servavit; ab ipsis
Romanis Romam Gallica servat avis."

† Hist. iii. 71.

excavations were made, remains of them would be discovered. Thus then in the words of Milton—

> " There the Capitol thou seest
> Above the rest lifting his stately head
> On the Tarpeian Rock, her citadel
> Impregnable."

Before leaving the subject of the Capitol, attention should be directed to another very interesting

THE MAMERTINE PRISON

part of it—the Mamertine Prison, which lies below us on the left hand, at the north-west extremity or corner of the Forum. While I was

standing on the steps of the Capitol, and in-
quiring my way of an Italian to this spot, he
took the opportunity of picking my pocket of
my handkerchief. I have called it the Mamertine
Prison, but Dungeon or Dungeons would be a
more appropriate name. It is a terrible place.
It is underground in what was once the side of
the hill on the south face of the Capitol. It consists of two subterranean chambers or vaults, into
which you now descend by stone stairs ; but
anciently there were no steps leading to the lower
dungeon, but the unhappy victims were let down
into it through a hole in the roof, which still
exists. It is difficult to make out at first sight
whether these dungeons are cut out of the solid
rock or built of enormous blocks of stone in the
style of Etruscan architecture. At all events there
is no doubt that they are an Etruscan work, and
are generally attributed to Ancus Martius. But
others think that Servius Tullius ought to have
the honour of being considered the builder of this
horrible gaol. Not however that it is now used
as such. Probably it was commenced by the first-
named king and enlarged by the second, from
whom it took the name of Tullianum—for it was
not called the Mamertine until the Middle Ages,

and for what reason it is difficult to say. The small Church of S. Guiseppe dei Falguami now stands above it, on the ground which, in the course of ages, has been heaped up against the declivity of the hill. That it was originally high above the level of the Forum is not only plain to the eye, by comparing the excavated portion of the Forum—of which I shall speak presently—with its present surface; but is also proved by the fact that frequent mention is made by the classic writers of some stairs leading up to it called *Gœmoniœ*, from which ordinary criminals were thrown and killed, just as state criminals were hurled from the Tarpeian Rock. Tacitus (Hist. iii. 74) mentions that the mutilated headless body of Flavius Sabinus was exposed in the Gæmoniæ stairs after his murder by the partisans of Vitellius, and there also the dead body of Sejanus, the profligate minister of Tiberius, was thrown after his execution. It was in the lowest of these dungeons that Jugurtha, the Numidian king, was starved to death. Plutarch tells us that on being let down into its gloomy depths he exclaimed, either in madness or in irony—" How cold, Romans, is this bath of yours !" And it was in this prison that the accomplices of Catiline in his great conspiracy

were confined after they had been arrested, and
here they were put to death by the order of the
Senate.

But in the eyes of the Roman Catholic a still
deeper interest attaches to this prison ; for, according to tradition, St. Peter was confined in it in the
reign of Nero. The story is that the Apostle here
converted the gaoler and several other fellow
prisoners, and that, in order to obtain water to
baptize them, he created a miraculous spring in
the floor of the dungeon. I can bear witness to
the existence of this spring, and to the excellence
of the water, however sceptical I may be about
its origin. A picture over an altar by the side
of the wall commemorates the baptism ; and, as
the candle of the monk who showed us the prison
shone upon it, I thought of the story of the gaoler
at Philippi, who sprang forward trembling with
the cry, " Sirs, what must I do to be saved ? "

But we are now on the top of the tower, the
sky is of unclouded brilliancy, and the only draw-
back is that the sun is rather too hot. For this
reason it is better to ascend either early in the
morning or shortly before sunset, when there is
not only less heat, but less haze in the distance.
We are looking towards the east, or rather, to
speak accurately, south-east.

Immediately below us is one of the most interesting spots in Rome. It is the Forum—an
irregular oblong space about a third of a mile in
length, which runs in a south-easterly direction
from the foot of the Capitol. How many asso

THE FORUM.

ciations crowd upon the mind as the eye rests
on this world-famous scene! We fancy still to
hear

" The immortal accents flow,
And still the eloquent air breathes—burns with Cicero."

Here was enacted the terrible tragedy of Virginia,

c 2

who was murdered by her father to save her from outrage worse than death at the hands of Appius Claudius the Decemvir. Here Antony pronounced that oration over the dead body of the murdered Cæsar, with which Shakespeare has made us all familiar; and this was the scene of the fiercest struggles between the Patricians and Plebeians, during which the latter slowly but surely fought their way to an equality of rights and power in the State. It was once the busiest spot in the greatest city in the world, surrounded by shops, and the centre of public life at Rome; and now it is a deserted space of open ground, with nothing but a few pillars and fragments of ruins to attest its former glory.*

In modern times it has borne the name of *Il Campo Vaccino*, or the cattle market, because it was used as a sort of Roman Smithfield; and it is curious that Virgil, in his description of its state at the time when he represents Æneas and his companions as landing in Italy, says that he then saw herds of cattle wandering in (what was after-

---

* There were altogether eleven Forums in Rome, called respectively Romanum, Magnum, Cæsaris, Augusti, Nervæ, Trajani, Ahenobarbi, Boarium, Pistorum, Gallorum, and Pistorum. The first-named was *the* Forum.

wards) the Forum, and heard them bellowing in
the part called the Carinæ, which lay between the
south of the Forum and the Esquiline Hill.

One of the most interesting parts of the Forum
is the Rostra, which was the platform from which
the Roman orators used to address the people,
and it derived its name at the conclusion of the
great Latin war from the beaks of ships, called
rostra, taken from the enemy in a sea-fight. These
were fixed to its sides, and projected from them as
a trophy of victory. A portion of the Rostra, which
was of a curvilinear form, has been within the last
few years uncovered, and as we stand on the tower
of the Capitol it lies directly below us, a little on
the left, close to the Arch of Septimius Severus.*
In front of it used to stand the Duilian column—
a pillar ornamented with the brazen beaks of ships
taken by Caius Duilius in the first naval victory
gained by the Romans over the Carthaginians, about
five centuries after the foundation of the city. A
fragment of the inscription on the pedestal is still
preserved in the museum of the Capitol on the
pillar as restored by Michael Angelo.

---

* There was another platform or *Rostra* at the opposite end
of the Forum, erected by Julius Cæsar, and it was there that
Antony pronounced his oration over the body of Cæsar.

When I use the term "uncovered" I ought to
explain that the whole of the Forum was until a
few years ago covered with earth and rubbish, the
accumulation of *débris* for centuries, to the depth
of about fifteen feet. But a small portion—alas!
only a small portion—has been now excavated, and
the ancient surface has been laid bare. A solitary
pillar stands close to the Rostra, which Byron
apostrophises as—

"Thou nameless column with a buried base;"

for in his time the base was covered with earth,
and there was nothing to indicate its history. But
now the earth has been cleared away, and an
inscription was found on its plinth or base which
tells us that it was erected by Smaragdas, the
exarch of Italy, A.D. 608, in honour of Phocas, one
of the most execrable of the Roman emperors, who
died A.D. 610.

The most interesting discovery made during the
excavations was the laying bare the pavement of
the ancient *Via Sacra,* or *Sacred Way,* which led to
the Capitol, and also part of the Clivus Capitolinus,
along which the Roman generals marched when
they enjoyed the honour of a triumph, and along
which also the miserable captives followed in sad
procession, to meet the death to which they were

by the pitiless law of Roman warfare foredoomed. The course taken by the triumphal *cortège* seems to have been this. The victorious general, after halting his army in the Campus Martius until he received permission from the Senate to enter the walls, marched from the plain into the city through the Porta Carmentalis, at the western extremity of the Capitoline Hill, and advanced past the Arch of Janus Quadrifrons along the road between the Palatine and the Aventine (now the *Via di Cerchi*). He then turned to the left into the road that runs between the Palatine and the Cœlian Hills, which was called the *Via Triumphalis* (now Via S. Gregory), and emerged into the Via Sacra, near the point where the Arch of Constantine now stands. Then turning to the left he marched straight to the Capitol from the south.

The pavement of the Via Sacra consists of large flat polygonal blocks of stone-like slate, irregularly laid down, and it looks almost as perfect as if it had been constructed yesterday instead of being more than 2,000 years old. The Via Sacra passes straight up the Forum, and close to the Arch of Septimius Severus it is joined by the Clivus Capitolinus, which went under that arch and formerly led to the Capitol ; but it is now covered except

for a small space by the modern road that winds
up the ascent.

Immediately below us, on the left, at the foot of
the Capitol, behind the arch of Septimius Severus,
are the remains of the Temple of Concord—memor-

ARCH OF SEPTIMIUS SEVERUS.

able as having been erected (I speak now of the
original temple) by Camillus, in the middle of the
fourth century before Christ, to commemorate the
termination of the contest between the Patricians

and Plebeians by opening one of the consulships
to the latter, and according to them other political
privileges.

The three beautiful columns supporting an
entablature at a little distance to the right of the
Temple of Concord (looking towards the Forum)
are supposed by some antiquaries to belong to the
Temple of Vespasian, by others to the Temple of
Saturn. But it is clear that the temple, whatever
it might be, of which they formed part, occupied
the site of some older building, for along the frieze
of the entablature are sculptured in large size
the letters *ESTITVER*, showing that this was a
restoration. It seems to me that Canina is right
in calling it the Temple of Vespasian.

Near this is a more imposing ruin, consisting of
an Ionic portico of eight columns, which, on good
authority, is supposed to be the remains of the
Temple of Saturn, where the Ærarium or Roman
Treasury was kept.

In front of the Temple of Saturn, but separated
from it by the modern road which now leads up
to the Capitol from the south, and which, as I
have said before, is almost fifteen feet higher than
the old bottom of the Forum, is the site of the
Basilica Julia, the existence of which was not

known until the recent excavations were made. But I had better describe what is meant by a basilica.

The ancient basilicas were courts of justice as well as places of business, and have an especial interest for us, as they were the models of the

BASILICA OF CONSTANTINE.

early Christian churches, and, in fact, a great many of them were converted into churches when Christianity became the prevalent religion of the

Roman empire. Let me explain the construction of these basilicas, and you will at once see the resemblance between them and our modern churches, and how suitable they were for transformation into Christian temples.

The basilica consisted of a lofty hall, with two rows of pillars running from one end to the other, parallel and near to the side walls, so as to leave between the two rows a wide vacant space in the body of the building. Here you will observe we have the nave and two side aisles. These pillars supported an entablature, above which were windows which admitted light into the hall, like the clerestory windows of our cathedrals.

At one end of the hall, between the two rows of pillars, was a' semicircular space called the *tribune*, where the judges sat and the trials were held. The public used the body of the hall for walking about and gossiping, just as is the case in Westminster Hall now. In this tribune, when the basilica was converted into a church, was placed the altar, and this was the origin of the modern chancel. Still, however, an important feature is wanting—namely, the cross-like form by which architecture symbolises our faith in the Crucified. Of this there was no trace in the old basilicas, for

the aisles ran straight on, as I have said, from end
to end. But the Christian architects attained their
object by throwing out on each side, near the
tribune, a transept, which was sometimes used as
a side chapel, as may be seen in that most perfect
specimen of a basilica transformed into a church
—the Santa Maria Maggiore at Rome. I know
no church that pleased me more than this. It has
a noble simplicity and grandeur, which is quite
refreshing in contrast with the elaborate ornament
and profusion of detail which so often, in my
opinion, encumbers rather than adorns the interior
of churches. Here, however, the continuity of the
grand lines of pillars was unfortunately broken
by the Popes Sixtus V. and Benedict XIV., who
took away two on each side and threw an arch
over the vacant spaces to form the two side chapels
—each a miracle of costly beauty, but not sufficiently harmonizing with the simplicity of the rest
of the building.

To return, however, to the Basilica Julia. The
site, as I said before, has been excavated, and the
broken bases of the lines of pillars that once supported the roof may be seen; but beyond these, and
a few fragments of stone and marble, not a vestige
of the building remains. I may here mention

that the site of a much larger basilica has lately
been excavated in the Forum of Trajan, at the
north end of which stands the well-known Column
of Trajan, which was the model of the Napoleon

TRAJAN'S COLUMN.

Column in the Place Vendôme in Paris. This
basilica was called Ulpia, from the family name
of Trajan, and was of immense size. Only
about a third of it has yet been excavated; and

there seems no chance of uncovering more, as the rest of the site is occupied by streets and houses.

Just beyond, that is, at the south-east end of the Basilica Julia, stand three most beautiful pillars, the sole relics of a building the name and destination of which have been a fertile subject of dispute amongst antiquaries. Some think that they belonged to the Temple of Jupiter Stator, or Jupiter the Stayer of Flight; others attribute them to the Temple of Minerva Chalcidice, built by Augustus; others to the Temple of the Dioscuri, that is, Castor and Pollux; while others have thought that they were part of a Græcostasis or hall, in which the ambassadors of friendly nations were received and entertained by the Senate. But, however critics may differ as to the nature of the building of which they formed part, there is—there can be—but one opinion as to their matchless beauty. I first saw them by moonlight as I wandered in the Forum on the night of the day when I arrived in Rome, and I never shall forget the impression they made upon me. There they stood, those three tall, graceful columns, rising above the wreck of ages—apparently so frail that a slight effort would push them down, and yet

they had survived the vicissitudes of time, the
storm, and the battle; and, perhaps more destructive than all, the hand of the spoiler—for it is
well known that the ancient buildings of Imperial
Rome were used as a sort of quarry in the Middle
Ages, out of which palaces and churches were built,
or, at all events, furnished with their principal
ornaments.

We have now glanced at the principal objects
in so much of the Forum as has yet been excavated; but before we leave it you will naturally
ask, Why is not more—why is not the whole of it
disinterred? At present a road runs along the
surface of the accumulated earth that hides it
from our view, and it is one of the thoroughfares
to the Colosseum, and the public walks and the
groves on the Cœlian Hill. But this would be no
obstacle, for the road could be carried along the
old bottom of the Forum as easily as on the top of
the accumulated deposit, and the expense would
be trifling. A body of English railway navigators
would clear the whole space in a month, and who
can say what treasures of antiquity might not be
brought to light, which now lie buried a few yards
beneath our feet? Under any other European
government, except perhaps that of Turkey, this

would have been done long ago ; and it does seem
to be a disgrace to Rome that the whole of this
spot, the cradle of her ancient glory, has not been
excavated and thoroughly explored. It is quite
possible that statues might be discovered that
would rival the Laocoon, which was dug up in a
vineyard on the Esquiline Hill, or the Dying
Gladiator, which was found amongst the ruins in
the gardens of Sallust.

In fact, there is no saying what marble "nuggets"
might not turn up if the Pope would only allow
the "diggings" to go on there ; for it needs little
sagacity to predict that in such a locality something of value would be discovered.*

Look now from the tower, on which I suppose that
we are standing, across the Forum to its south-east
end, and you will see a marble arch, under which
the road I have mentioned, the Via Sacra, runs.
This is the Arch of Titus, erected by the Senate
after the death of that emperor, to commemorate

* Addison says, in his Remarks on Italy, that the Jews were
so confident of finding all kinds of valuable treasures in the bed
of the Tiber, that they offered to the Pope to cleanse it, and
make a new channel for the river in the meantime. One of the
latest found works of art in the Tiber is a beautiful figure in
bronze, now in Berlin, called *Der betende Knabe;* or, the
Praying Boy.

the conquest of Jerusalem. It consists of an arch of white marble, not at all unlike at a distance the Marble Arch which stands at the north-east corner of Hyde Park. The bas-reliefs sculptured upon it

ARCH OF TITUS.

are particularly interesting; for they represent a procession carrying the spoils of Jerusalem, and amongst them the golden seven-branched candlestick of the Temple, which is said to have been

D

lost in the Tiber at the defeat of Maxentius by
Constantine.   It is the only authentic representa-

SPOILS FROM JERUSALEM.

tion of this sacred object known to exist; and it
is impossible to gaze on it without feelings of deep
emotion, as it calls up before our memory the history of the Temple, and its destruction in the last
terrible siege of Jerusalem.   Beyond this arch, in
the same direction, at less than a furlong's distance, rise the mighty ruins of the Colosseum, or
Flavian Amphitheatre.   It was commenced by
Vespasian on the site of an artificial lake constructed by Nero,* and it was afterwards continued
by Titus, and finished by Domitian.   It is of an

* Hic ubi conspicui venerabilis Amphitheatri
  Erigitur moles, stagna Neronis erant.
                                        Mart. De Spect. Ep. ii. v. 5.

oval form, and when complete was able to contain
87,000 spectators.

I frequently visited these ruins, but on two
occasions the difference and contrast of my visits
were so great, that I should like to describe them.

COLOSSEUM.

The one was by day, and the other by night. The
former occasion was on a Sunday afternoon; the
sun shone brilliantly, though the unclouded sky
made it unpleasantly hot. When I entered the
Colosseum not a soul was there but myself, and
I stood beside a crucifix, or image of the Virgin,

I forget which, which is placed in one of the
vaulted passages that forms the principal entrance
at this end. At that moment a party of Roman
peasants, both men and women, dressed in their
very picturesque costume, came into the Colosseum,
and each knelt and prayed, and kissed the image
before they passed into the interior. In the centre
of the arena stands a large wooden crucifix, and
here also several of the party knelt, and then
pressed their foreheads across the cross.

I could not help thinking of the contrast between this scene and such acts of worship, and
the scenes of horror that had been so often enacted
there. I thought of the cry of *" Christianos ad
leones !"* with which those walls had re-echoed,
when whilst every seat was crowded with an eager
multitude, not of men only, but women—of all
the rank and fashion and beauty of Imperial Rome
—the Christian martyrs stood on that very spot
awaiting the spring of the wild beasts, whose
roar was heard in the subterraneous dens where
they were raging for their prey.

The other occasion to which I allude was when
I went with a friend to the Colosseum at night,
just as the moon was rising above the east wall of
the ruins. We were challenged as we approached

by the French sentry who is stationed there, but
were allowed to enter the arena. The silence was
unbroken by any sound, except that of the owls,
which hooted in the most orthodox manner, and
the whole scene was in perfect harmony with the
idea of the fallen majesty of Rome. The reason
why a sentry keeps guard at the Colosseum is on
account of the assassinations and robberies which
have been committed in its gloomy recesses. A
story is told of an English traveller who one night
visited it, and as he was coming out through a
vaulted passage suddenly missed his watch, and
seeing a person near with a watch-chain hanging
from his pocket, he seized it, thinking that it was
his own, and that the stranger was the robber.
On getting to his hotel, he discovered to his
amazement that his own watch was on the table
where he had left it, and that he himself was the
robber in having forcibly taken another man's
watch. Next morning he hurried to the police-
office, and there he found a respectable priest, who
had just been piteously complaining that he had
been robbed on the preceding night at the Colosseum, of his watch, by a Garibaldista Inglese!

But let us now leave what I may call the fore-
ground of the picture before us, and turn our at-

tention to the higher ground that surrounds it.
We will take the six other hills of Rome, in order
as they meet the eye, for you will remember that
we are supposed to be standing on the Capitoline,
which forms the seventh.

That mound-shaped hill on the extreme right,
beneath which the Tiber rolls its muddy stream to
the Mediterranean, is the Aventine. It is so close
to the river that there is barely room for the carriage road which leads to the Porta S. Paolo, outside of which, at the distance of about a mile from
the Aventine, has been recently rebuilt the mag-
nificently decorated church of S. Paolo, on the site
of the former venerable church of the same name,
which was destroyed by fire in 1823. On the
summit of the Aventine are two churches, with
convents adjoining them. The one nearest us is
the Church of S. Sabina, which belongs to a
Dominican convent, where the present Pope once
resided, and the trees and shrubs which you see
there are part of the gardens of the monastery, in
which one of the monks pointed out to us a
lemon-tree said to have been planted by S. Domi-
nico, the founder of the Inquisition, himself. Of
course ladies are never admitted within the precincts of the convent, and therefore they must

take on trust what they are told of the interior. But, in truth, there is nothing to tell. There is a curious old cloister in a sadly dilapidated and dirty condition, surrounded by the cells of the brethren, and a garden overrun with weeds, and utterly neglected. As we entered the convent, we saw basins of what looked like very good soup, doled out to some hungry beggars, who get their dinner there every day for the trouble of walking up the ascent for it. The church contains a very fine painting of the Virgin and Child by Sasso Ferrato.

The other church on the Aventine is that of S. Alessio, about which I believe there is nothing remarkable. At all events, I am not competent to speak of it on my own authority, as I did not think it worth while to go inside.

But what was the early history of the Aventine? Among all the Seven Hills of Rome it is entitled to precedence, for here, according to the old tradition, as it is beautifully told by Virgil, King Latinus held his court when Æneas and his companions landed at the mouth of the Tiber after the capture of Troy. Let me try and bring before you a picture of that old-world time, as it is drawn by the poet.

Anxious to conciliate the friendship of Latinus,

Æneas sends an embassy, consisting of a hundred
of his followers, with presents to the king. They
set out on their journey, and as they approach the
city of the Latins, they see the inhabitants en-
gaged outside the walls in warlike games. The
arrival of the strangers attracts attention, and King
Latinus orders them to be brought before him.
He is seated on his ancestral throne, in a lofty
building with a portico of a hundred columns,
which is at once a temple and a banqueting-hall,
adorned with statues and trophies, and surrounded
by trees. The king interrogates the Trojans as to
the cause of their coming to Italy, and when told
of the sufferings and exploits of Æneas, and pre-
sented with a sceptre which had once belonged to
old Priam, he expresses an ardent desire to make
the acquaintance, and grasp the hand, of the Trojan
hero. And not to be outdone in generosity, he
sends back the strangers with three hundred
horses, decked in golden trappings, as his gift ; and
for Æneas himself, he sends a chariot drawn by
two coursers of celestial race.

It was on the Aventine that Remus stood, while
his brother Romulus was stationed on the Palatine,
to take the auguries that were to determine which
of the two was to be the founder of the future

city. Possibly owing to the gloomy tradition of Remus's murder, or from some other cause, the Aventine seems to have borne an unlucky reputation. It was never during the time of the Republic included in the precincts of the city, or Pomœrium,* as it was called ; and to it on more than one occasion, the Plebeians retired in sullen discontent during their long contest with the Patricians for equality of rights. It was here that Camillus dedicated a temple to Juno, after the capture of Veii, and here was the Temple of Diana, common to all the Latin tribes, where Caius Gracchus, just before his death, fled for refuge, and, stung by the ingratitude of the Romans, prayed that they might never be free.

* The Pomœrium, *i.e.* the *post mœrium* (murus) was a symbolical line marked by small stone pillars (*cippi*) which might be either within or without the actual walls ; but within its circumference alone could the city auspices be held. The *Pomœrium* of Rome was increased on two or three occasions ; but only by those who had enlarged the boundary of her dominion by foreign conquest, and after solemnly consulting the augurs to see whether the gods were favourable. This fell to the lot of Sylla, Julius Cæsar, and the Emperor Claudius. The Aventine was first included in the Pomœrium in the reign of the last-named Emperor ; but it was surrounded by a wall as early as the time of Ancus Martius, when, according to Livy, it was assigned as the quarter for the population of some captured cities (Livy i. 32).

The only fragments of the old wall of Servius
Tullius until lately known to exist were those on
the Aventine, near the Church of St. Prisca ; but
recently, in clearing away the ground for the
Central Railway Station, near the Baths of Dio-

OLD WALLS OF ROME.

cletian, some far finer remains have been discovered, consisting of immense blocks of dark
stone. With true Vandal contempt, however, for
relics of antiquity, these' blocks have not only
been detached and dislocated, but their primitive
forms have been destroyed by the chisel, in order,

I suppose, to make them available for the romantic purpose of a railway station !

Between the Aventine Hill and the spot where we are now standing, there are several objects of interest, which it will be worth while to point out.

CLOACA MAXIMA.

In the hollow below runs the Cloaca Maxima, the great sewer of Rome, and the oldest now existing in the world, for it dates from the time of Tarquinius Priscus.

It was not, however, exactly what we now mean by the word sewer, though it agrees with the ancient signification of the term. It was originally an open channel or water-course for three-fifths of its length, cut for the purpose of draining the marshy ground that lay under and in the neighbourhood of the Palatine Hill. As it approached the Tiber, it became a subterraneous tunnel, and it still pours its water into the river a short distance below, that is, to the west of the bridge called the Ponte Rotto, of which I will speak by-and-by. . I had some difficulty in finding this famous work of what may be called the Commissioners of Sewers of ancient Rome ; for the Tiber was so swollen, that its waters had risen higher than the mouth of the Cloaca Maxima, and completely hid it from view ; and when I inquired for the course of the sewer, which I knew could be seen and traced at some little distance from the bank, nobody seemed to know what I meant, but I was told the whole neighbourhood was called Cloaca Massima. Originally, before the foundation of Rome, the ground at the foot of the Palatine Hill, between it and the Tiber, and extending over the whole space afterwards occupied by the Forum, was a marshy swamp, in which was a large pool of water, called the Lake of Iuturna. This swamp was known by the name of the *Velabrum*, an Etruscan word ; and it was to drain this that the Cloaca Maxima was formed.* At its eastern extremity, my attention was directed to it by seeing a man stoop down in a hollow recess, and fill a jug with water, which he drank. I thought it an odd place to go to for a draught of water, as this was really the Cloaca Maxima, or Great Sewer ; but it proved to be a limpid stream of fresh running water, which looked perfectly fresh and good, although I was too much under the influence of my imagination to have the courage to taste it. Close beside it, some women were employed in washing clothes. To give an idea of the stupendous nature of this work, I may mention what Strabo says, namely, that a waggon loaded with hay might have passed through the Cloaca. The covered part extended

---

* Some antiquaries confine the *Velabrum* to the low ground between the Forum and the Tiber, so as not to include the Forum. Propertius mentions it, El. iv. 10 :—

"Quâ Velabra suo stagnabant flumine, quâque
Nauta per Albanas velificabat aquas."

See also Tacit Hist. i. 27, who places it between the Palace of Tiberius (on the Palatine) and the Golden Milestone, which we know stood at the head of the Forum, close to the Temple of Saturn.

from a point opposite the church of S. Georgio, in the Velabro, to the river; but the upper portion of its course was an open drain. For the reason I have mentioned—namely, the flood in the Tiber —I was not able to examine the tunnel; but it is said that, in consequence of the rise in the bed of the river, the channel has been considerably choked up.

Close beside the recess in which flows the limpid stream, stands the square four-arched edifice of *Janus Quadrifrons*. It is pierced in each front with an arch, forming a vault in the centre, and stands in what was the Forum Boarium, or Cattle Market.* During the Middle Ages, a fortress was erected by the family of the Frangipani on the top of it, some remains of which may still be seen. Between the Janus Quadrifrons and the Tiber is the celebrated Temple of Vesta—that beautiful little circular building, surrounded by pillars, of which there are so many drawings and models. It is a very favourite form of inkstand, and one of the commonest objects in the shops of

---

* At the western extremity of this was the very ancient Porta Mugonia (the Lowing or Bellowing Gate) in the old wall of Romulus, the name of which sufficiently indicates its proximity to the Cattle Market.

Page 62.

TEMPLE OF VESTA

Rome. It stands in a miserably dirty and neglected neighbourhood, and no care seems to be
taken of it beyond that of surrounding it by an
iron railing. The ugly tiled roof is, of course,
modern; but nothing can destroy the effect of its
proportions and shape. I am afraid it cannot be
identified with the Temple of Vesta, so interesting
to every classical scholar as the place mentioned
by Horace, in his amusing description of a walk
he took one day, in which he was pestered by
a troublesome fellow, who claimed acquaintance
with him, and whom he could not shake off.* A
few yards from the Temple of Vesta was the
Temple of Fortuna Virilis, now converted into a
church, but still distinctly a relic of antiquity, as
may be seen by its Ionic columns and entablature.
The temple was originally built in the days of the
kings, but was afterwards restored.

Just beyond this is a curious old house, which
seems to be made up of shreds and patches of
antiquities; but its interest chiefly depends upon
the fact that it was the residence of Cola Nicholas
Rienzi, the tribune—" the last of the Roman pa-

---

* Tacitus mentions (Ann. xv. 41) that the *delubrum Vestæ*
was destroyed by the great fire in Nero's time. This was probably the shrine or temple of Vesta of which Horace speaks.

triots," as he has been called by Gibbon—who, after enjoying regal power at Rome, and the honour of an actual coronation, was massacred in a tumult, A.D. 1354.

Immediately in front of Rienzi's house is the Ponte Rotto, or Broken Bridge, so called because half of it was swept away by a flood soon after it was built in the sixteenth century, and the stone arches so destroyed have never been replaced, but a flat iron bridge has been made, which joins the left bank of the river to that part of the stone-work still remaining; so that the bridge is made up for one half of its length of iron and for the other half of stone. It stands where the old Pons Palatinus formerly crossed the river, and where the dead body of the murdered monster Elagabalus was thrown by the Prætorian Guards. Michael Angelo was to have been its architect; but, owing to some miserable jealousy against the great man, the work was taken from him and given to a person called Bigio, who was wholly incompetent for the task, and the result was that in five years half of it was washed away.

Speaking of bridges, I may mention that there were eight in ancient Rome, including the Pons Milvius, about a mile to the north of the

modern city. There are now six, including the
Ponte Molle, which corresponds to the Pons
Milvius. The oldest of all was the *Pons Sublicius*,
so called from its resting on wooden piles. It was
just under the Aventine, and it was here that,
according to the legend, Horatius Cocles singly
withstood the onset of the Etruscan army under
King Porsena, until the Romans broke down the
bridge behind him, when he flung himself into the
river and escaped. Here, too, it was that Clælia,
a Roman virgin who had been sent with other
ladies as a hostage to Porsena, plunged into the
Tiber, followed by her companions, and swam
safely across to Rome. It was a gallant act,
although I am afraid contrary to international law.
Porsena, however, behaved like a gentleman, and
when the runaway Clælia was restored to him
he sent her back with a very complimentary
message.

A little higher up the river, beyond the Ponte
Rotto, is the Isola di Tevera, or Island of the
Tiber, which, according to the old legend at Rome,
owed its origin to the popular hatred of the
Tarquins. For the story is that when the last
king of that race was expelled, the Campus
Martius, which was his private domain, was con-

fiscated to the State ; but the people, abhorring the
idea of using the corn that had grown on his
estate, cut down the crop and threw it in basket-
loads into the Tiber. As these floated down the
stream, some of them, meeting with impediments,
remained stationary, and so formed a nucleus for
the future island which formed itself around them.
Upon it, at the beginning of the third century before Christ, was founded the Temple of Æsculapius,
supposed to be represented now by the Hospital of
San Giovanni. During a plague at Rome an
embassy was sent to Epidamnus to bring an image
of Æsculapius to the city, in obedience to the
advice of the Sybilline Books. On their arrival
in the Tiber, a serpent glided from the ship and
hid itself amongst the reeds of the island. The
Romans thought that this was the god Esculapius
himself *in proprià personâ*, and they built the
Temple which I have mentioned, and cut the
island into the rough shape of a vessel, which it
still retains.

The next of the hills before us is the Palatine—
it lies a little to our right, that is, south-west of
the tower of the Capitol. It is almost square in
form, but the western and southern sides are longer
than those on the north and east. Steeper and more

CÆSAR'S PALACE, PALATINE HILL.   Page 67.

abrupt than any of the other hills, except at the southern end of the east side, where a lane called Via Polveriera, or Dusty Road (and it is very dusty), leads up to a monastery and a nunnery, you may walk round the whole of it in half an hour. The monastery is called St. Bonaventura, and the lane I have mentioned separates it from a nunnery—a red-brick building like a modern villa, which in fact it formerly was. It is known as the Villa Spada, or Villa Mills, from the name of an Englishman to whom it formerly belonged. It is perched up there in very questionable taste, and does not at all harmonize with the locality. Around the monastery and nunnery are vineyards and gardens; those on the right bearing the name of *Orti Farnesiani*, for the Palatine belongs, or at all events did belong, to the Farnese family, now represented by the King of Naples. The highest top of the Palatine Hill is on the north-west, and consists of a large level platform or terrace, where there is a wild, badly-kept garden swarming with lizards. I spent part of a sunny afternoon there, and the ground was quite alive with these merry little fellows, darting from beneath my foot at every step I took. The vast ruins of the Palace of the Cæsars lie chiefly on

the west side, and enormous substructions of
vaulted stone work cover the whole of that side,
forming an irregular face to the hill, with the road
called Via di Cerchi running along the base and
leading from the Velabro to the Porta S. Sebastiano, and the Appian Way. On the site of this
road, or just on the opposite side between the
Palatine and the Aventine, was the Circus Maximus, or what was called the Murcian Valley. It
is said to have owed its origin to Tarquinius
Priscus, and became afterwards the largest and
most splendid of all the places in Rome, devoted
to chariot races, sham fights, and other public
games, of which the people were passionately fond.
To give an idea of its size I may mention that
it is said to have been capable of holding 150,000
spectators.

Nothing can be imagined more utterly dreary and
desolate than the mass of ruins on the Palatine.
It is hopeless to attempt to disentangle them, and
to try and make out the original distinction of the
different parts. Some of the huge vaulted recesses
are now used as hay-lofts, and in one place I came
upon what I suppose is a modern Roman brewery,
if I may judge by the vats and pans I saw there.

The whole scene is fairly described by Lord Byron in the following lines :—

> " Cypress and ivy, weed and wall-flower, grown
> Matted and massed together, hillocks heaped
> On what were chambers, arch crushed, columns strown
> In fragments, choked up vaults, and frescoes steeped
> In subterranean damps, where the owl peeped
> Deeming it midnight :—temples, baths, or halls?
> Pronounce who can ; for all that learning reaped
> From her research hath been, that there are walls—
> Behold the Imperial Mount! 'Tis thus the mighty falls."

Perhaps no spot in Rome is more fitted to make the spectator moralize than this—none more suggestive of melancholy thoughts of the littleness of human grandeur. It seems to realize Isaiah's prophecy concerning Babylon : " And their houses shall be full of doleful creatures ; and owls shall dwell there, and satyrs shall dance there." And yet this is the place Milton truly describes as once

> "Mount Palatine
> The imperial palace, compass huge, and high
> The structure, skill of noblest architects,
> With gilded battlements conspicuous far,
> Turrets and terraces and glittering spires."

If we may accept the legend of Æneas and his companions from Troy as containing any germ of

truth, it derives its name from a hamlet—proudly
called a city—settled at its base under Evander,
and a body of colonists from Arcadia, to which
the name of Palanteum was given, after a city in
Greece of the same name which they had left.
And it is curious to trace the change in the signi-
fications of words. The word Palace, which is
appropriated by us to the abodes of kings and
bishops, is derived from the lowly huts of these
Arcadian wanderers. And the change came about
thus : In after times the Palatine was covered by
mansions of wealthy Romans, and during the
Empire it was occupied by the magnificent dwell-
ing of the Cæsars. Hence these residences were,
from their situation, called *palatial*, and as that of
the Emperor eclipsed and swallowed up all the
rest, the term Palace was at last confined to it.

It is certain that it was the site of the infant
town of Romulus, and therefore the cradle of
Rome, which for some years did not extend beyond its precincts, and hence was sometimes
called *Roma Quadrata*. Here during the time of
the Republic was preserved what was known as
the House of Romulus ; and here was the fig-tree,
Ficus Ruminalis, under which, according to the
legend, the twin brothers were suckled by the

she-wolf. Here too, according to some authors, in a part called Velia, the situation of which is now unknown, stood the house of the consul P. Valerius Publicola in a commanding position, and built of stone, which made the jealous Romans believe that he was aspiring to sovereignty ; but when he lowered the *fasces* before them in token of homage to their authority, they were so pleased that they not only permitted him to retain the house, but gave him a piece of land there besides.*

As the city extended itself the Palatine became the favourite resort of the aristocracy of Rome, and we know that upon it were built the stately houses of the Gracchi, and Crassus, and Clodius, and Catiline, and Hortensius, and Cicero. Not a vestige of these mansions now remains. When Augustus had become master of Rome, he built here a residence for himself, and comprised within it the houses of Hortensius and Cicero and others. But the palace of the Emperor was struck by lightning, and therefore, in obedience to the superstitious idea of the Romans, it was pulled down, and a temple built on its site, which was conse-

* Bunsen places the Velia on the opposite side of the Forum at the south-east end.

crated to Jupiter, or as Suetonius tells us, to Apollo. Tiberius and Caligula both had palaces on the hill, and the latter Emperor threw a bridge over the *Velabrum*, the low ground between the Palatine and the Capitoline. But all former structures were eclipsed by the *Domus Aurea*, or Golden House of Nero, which was one of the wonders of the world. Suetonius gives a description of it, which is more like that of a town than a palace, for he says that it contained a lake like a sea, surrounded with buildings (the site afterwards of the Colosseum), and in its precincts were woods stocked with all kinds of animals, and vineyards, and arable and pasture land. Most likely it was what we should call a magnificent mansion or palace, with a park adjoining. It was from a terrace of the Golden House that Nero witnessed the conflagration of Rome, which he was believed to have caused, and there he chanted the song of the burning of Troy while the flames devoured three-fourths of the then existing city.

After the destruction of Rome by the Gauls it was rebuilt in haste, and with so little regard to its original form that even the lines of the sewers were either forgotten or not observed. The streets

sprang up narrow and crooked, crossing irregularly
the *cloacæ* below, and so they remained until the
great fire in the time of Nero, who issued the
most stringent regulations to secure uniformity
and symmetry. Augustus divided the city into
fourteen regions, now called *Rioni*, and Tacitus
tells us that only four of these escaped the conflagration. Of the rest, three were utterly destroyed, and in the seven others only a few houses
remained, and these were half consumed by fire.

The gorgeous palace of Nero was of course
pillaged by the barbarians who invaded Rome.
Genseric, the leader of the Vandals in the fifth
century, stripped it of immense treasures, and
sent off a shipload of statues, supposed to be
chiefly taken from the Golden House. But it
might have remained almost entire until our own
day if it had not been for the intestine quarrels and
sordid rapacity of the Romans themselves. In the
Middle Ages it was converted into a fortress, and
afterwards it was plundered of even its stones to
build palaces for popes, and cardinals, and princes,
until it became what it is now, a shapeless mass
of ruin, with cabbages and artichokes covering it as
with a funeral pall.

Latterly extensive excavations have been going

on in the Palatine, and the foundations of many
large buildings have been laid bare, as to which of
course antiquarian speculation has been busy in
assigning names and localities. It was somewhere
here that the caricature was discovered of a Christian worshipping the Saviour, with the head of an
ass, and the inscription under the figure was—

'Αλεξάμενος σέβετε (*i.e.* σέβεται) Θεόν.

On the south side of the Palatine, and divided
from it only by a road called the *Via di S. Gregorio*,
is the Mons Cœlius, or Cœlian Hill, which affords
one of the pleasantest walks in Rome. It is low
in height, and its gentle slope is covered with
trees, which make it a favourite promenade. At
the time of the foundation of the city it was
called Querqueta, or the Hill of Oaks, and it is
said to have derived its name of Cœlius from
Cœles Vibenna, an Etruscan chieftain, who seems
to have held it with his followers in the earliest
times of Rome, but nothing authentic is known
about him.* It was walled round by Tullus Hos-

---

* See Tacit. Ann IV. 65. The level space between the Forum
and the Velabrum was always called the *Tuscus Vicus*, or the
Tuscan quarter, just as in London there is a place called the
Savoy because the residence of a former Count of Savoy once
stood there in the reign of Henry III.

tilius, who after the destruction of Alba Longa, settled a body of the conquered inhabitants on this hill, and fixed there his own royal residence. Many ruins are scattered about the hill, but in such a state of dilapidation that nothing can be made out respecting them. Some are supposed to be the remains of the *Vivarium*, or menagerie, where the wild beasts were kept for the gladiatorial shows and Christian martyrdoms. We know that here stood the Temples of Faunus, and Bacchus, and Claudius, a barrack of gladiators (*Gladiatorum Ludus*), and many other buildings, but they were all almost entirely destroyed by a great fire in the time of Tiberius; and Tacitus tells us that the abject Senate proposed that the hill should afterwards be called *Mons Augustus*, out of compliment to the Emperor, because his statue had alone escaped the fire unscathed.

On the south-western side of the Cœlian hill are two churches and monasteries, one of which has an especial interest for Englishmen. It is the church and monastery of S. Gregorio, on the site where once stood the family residence of Gregory the Great, the Pope who sent St. Augustine, at the end of the sixth century, to Britain, to convert our Saxon forefathers to the Christian faith. "In 596, during an interval of peace with the Lombards, he despatched Augustine, provost of his own monastery, with a party of monks, to preach the Gospel in England, and about the same time he desired Candidius, defender of the Papal estates in Gaul, to buy up English captive youths, and to place them in monasteries, with a view of training them for the conversion of their country-men." *

The situation of the church is very beautiful. The entrance is through a square court-yard, round which runs a covered corridor, where there are several monuments and epitaphs, and a marble slab at the gate tells the traveller to stop and think of what Gregory did for England. While I was there the monks were chanting vespers in the choir of the church, and a French soldier and myself constituted the whole of the congregation. And here I may mention that in none of the numerous churches that I visited while I was at Rome—except on Sunday—did I see more than three or four persons at their devotions. In many cases they were quite empty. But I do not state this by way of reproach, for assuredly we have no right to cast in the teeth of Roman Catholics the

* Robertson's History of the Christian Church, ii. p. 15.

paucity of attendance in their churches—*we* who
keep ours, with very few exceptions, closed six
days of the week, and only open some of our
cathedrals on the payment of a fee.

The other church on the Cœlian Hill is that of
S. Giovanni and S. Paolo,—St. John and St. Paul,
not the Apostles, but two officers of the Imperial
household, who were put to death in the reign of
Julian the Apostate. The spot where they suffered
martyrdom is indicated by a stone in the new
ground of the nave, surrounded by a low railing.
The adjoining convent belongs to the Passionist
monks, who wear in their coarse black cloaks the
figure of a heart, with the initials of Jesus Christ
and the letter P worked into it.

At the east end of the road which I have mentioned as dividing the Cœlian from the Palatine
Hill, and directly facing the Colosseum, stands
the noble Arch of Constantine, which was erected
to commemorate the decisive victory of that
emperor over his rival, Maxentius, at the Milvian
bridge, near Rome, which paved the way to the
establishment of Christianity as the prevalent
religion, and of which there is a noble fresco
in the Vatican, designed by Raphael, but not
executed by him. The bas-reliefs in the front

of the arch facing the Colosseum represent the
triumphant entry of Trajan into Rome, and those
on the opposite side, Trajan crowning the King of
Panthea, and other incidents of that emperor's
life. The reason why Trajan thus figures on the
archway is that it is composed of fragments taken
from one of the previously existing arches of that
emperor.

Let us now direct our attention to a large building, crowned with statues, which lies in a direct line
south of the Colosseum, on the south-eastern extremity of the Cœlian hill, and about a mile from
the watch tower on which we are standing. This
is the Lateran, the old palace of the popes, with its
church of San Giovanni, which bears on its front
the proud inscription—

" OMNIUM URBIS ET ORBIS ECCLESIARUM MATER ET CAPUT."

It is, I believe, what we should call the parish
church of Rome, and St. Peter's, in reality, is only
a chapel of ease. It derives its name from a
Roman Senator, Plautus Lateranus, whose house
occupied the site, and who was put to death by
Nero on the charge of being implicated in a conspiracy. Here the coronation of the new pope
takes place, as has been the custom for more than

1500 years, and the adjoining palace was for centuries the papal residence, before it was removed to the Vatican. I shall not attempt to describe the church further than by saying that it is a vast and noble building, with a nave and two aisles on each side, and aloft in niches along the nave are colossal figures of the Apostles, by Bernini, clothed in masses of flowing drapery, which is the characteristic of his style. It contains a side chapel belonging to the Corsini family, which exceeds in richness of ornament anything of the kind in Rome. The Lateran stands in a deserted part of Rome, inside, and within a stone throw of the walls. There are a very few houses near it, and before the principal entrance on the east is a wide open grass-covered space like a village common. From the terrace beside the wall, which is pleasantly shaded by trees, there is a most lovely view of the Campagna, and the distant Latin hills, which stretch along like the frame of a beautiful picture.

In this church are shown some famous relics ; one especially, the upper surface of the table on which the Last Supper is said to have been eaten ! It is kept in a closet in a corridor, fastened into the wall and covered with glass. I was much struck with the beautiful cloister of the Lateran.

The centre is a flower-garden, which when I was there was a perfect wilderness of roses. The open corridors that run round this are remarkable for the beautiful small Gothic pillars on the sides next the garden. They are ornamented with mosaics, and are twisted into spiral forms in the most graceful manner imaginable.

In these corridors they show you several curiosities; amongst others there is a flat marble slab, supported by four pillars, which are said to be of the exact height of our Saviour, and the legend is that no man can be found of precisely the same height. I tried it by standing under the slab, but I was just too short. The fact is, the height is six feet, and as I am not quite so tall, my failure afforded what will be considered, I suppose, another proof of the truth of the story.

Close to the Lateran is a building like a church, but it is, I believe, called a portico, in which is the *Scala Santa*, a flight of twenty-eight marble steps, said to have been those by which our Saviour descended from Pilate's judgment hall. They are protected by wooden planking, and up them the faithful crawl on their knees to a little chapel at the summit, which is full of relics, in the existence of which the fair sex must be content to believe without ocular proof, for no woman is allowed to enter it. For the benefit of those who do not like to perform the ceremony of walking on their knees (the only permitted mode of ascending the stairs), two flights of steps, one on each side, and parallel to the Sacred Stairs, lead up to the chapel, and by one of these I ascended, and descended by the other. At the bottom of the stairs, on the lowest step, the monk in attendance, who carried a money-box for contributions, showed me a little round hole, covered with glass, which he said contained a drop of our Saviour's blood.

On leaving the Scala Santa some old women pestered us for money on the plea that they had crawled up the stairs on their knees; but, as I had made up my mind never to give anything to a beggar in Rome, they were obliged to be satisfied with my good wishes, and the expression of my hope that the exercise had done them good.

We must now turn more to the left, that is, to the east, and looking in that direction the spectator will see a large church crowning the top of some elevated ground thickly built on with houses. That church is the church of S. Maria Maggiore, of which I have before spoken when I described the ancient basilicas, and that elevated ground is

F

the Esquiline Hill. It was originally called *Fagu-talis*, which means " covered with beeches," and sufficiently expresses its old sylvan appearance. The principal ruins there are those of the Baths of Titus, which are interesting from the remains of ancient frescoes, the colours of which are still vivid, in the ceiling of a corridor. They are said to be "the most perfect specimens of ancient paintings which have been preserved in Rome."* Nero's Golden House extended up this hill, striding across the valley where the Colosseum now stands, and occupying the site of the house and gardens of Mæcenas. In the later times of the Republic the Esquiline was a common cemetery of the poorer classes, and thought to be extremely unhealthy. Augustus Cæsar first put a stop to their burials, and converted the hill into a favourite residence of the Roman patricians.

Horace, who was a thorough courtier, and never lost an opportunity of offering the incense of flattery to the Emperor, tells us that the Es-quiline had just been made habitable, and formed a pleasant promenade—

" Nunc licet Esquiliis habitare salubribus, atque
Aggere in aprico spatiari."

* Murray's Handbook of Rome.

He represents the hill as formerly the haunt of witches, who searched there for noxious herbs, and he introduces two whom he calls Canidia and Sagana, busy at their incantations on the spot. Both are suddenly frightened, and as they run away Canidia's false teeth drop out, and Sagana's wig tumbles off. The Esquiline is perhaps the most extensive of the Seven Hills, but only a portion of it is now inhabited. The rest is a dreary desolation. I may mention that between the Church of S. Pietro in Vincolo, on one of its summits, and the Forum, there is a street which is said to be that in which the inhuman Tullia drove over the murdered body of her father, King Servius Tullius, and which afterwards bore the name of *Via Scelerata*, or Street of Infamy.

To the north-west of the Esquiline stands the Quirinal Hill, or as it is now called, Monte Cavallo. It derives its name from Quirites, an appellation of the Sabines; and at the time when the Palatine was occupied by Romulus it was inhabited by a Sabine settlement, and was the rival and enemy of Rome until, under Tatius, an union of the two people took place, and the name Quirites came to be applied to the whole, although it was always considered a less honourable title than

F 2

Romani. During the reign of the Republic, and indeed until the time of Trajan, the Quirinal and the Capitol formed parts of the same continuous ridge; but that emperor, in order to provide a sufficient space for the new Forum which he wished to establish, cut the ridge in two, and thus made two separate eminences, with a valley occupied by the Forum and Trajanum between them.

The broad top of this hill is occupied by the immense palace of the popes, called the Quirinal, with a garden of corresponding size attached to it. It was built in the sixteenth century, and is still from time to time inhabited by the Pope. In the desolate-looking piazza or square in front is a remarkable group of statuary—two colossal figures of men with horses, called Castor and Pollux. On the pedestal of one of these statues are engraved the words *Opus Phidiæ*, and on the other *Opus Praxitelis*—to signify that they were the works of those famous Greek sculptors. But I believe that there is not the slightest authority for this. They were found amongst the ruins of the Baths of Constantine, but are supposed to be of much older date than the reign of that emperor. The action of the figures is grand in the extreme, and I know no more striking *group* in Rome, although there are many individual statues which are finer.

HORSES ON MONTE CAVALLO, IN FRONT OF THE QUIRINAL.

Page 84.

We have now visited with the mind's eye six of
the hills of Rome—the Capitoline, the Aventine
the Palatine, the Cœlian, the Esquiline, and the
Quirinal ; and the next question is, which is the
seventh ?   I have already mentioned that there is
a doubt whether the Mons Viminalis ought not to
be considered rather as a part of the Esquiline
than as a separate hill ; and it is really so insignificant, and has so little interest attached to it, that
I am inclined not to raise it to the dignity of one
of the Seven Hills, but assume, in company with
very respectable authorities, that that honour
rather belongs to the Janiculum, which lies on the
other side of the Tiber, and is part of a hilly ridge
that rises out of the Campagna to the north-west
of Rome, about a mile and a half long.   Of this
ridge Monte Verde is the southern, and the
Vatican is the northern extremity.   Between it
and the river is the quarter called Trastevere,
bearing the same relation to Rome that the Surrey
side of the Thames does to London.   On the
Janiculum stands the very ancient church of S
Pietro in Montorio, close to the spot where, according to Roman Catholic tradition, St. Peter was
crucified.   Let us however now return to the left
bank of the Tiber, and before we finally dismiss

the Viminal let me mention that it was either upon
or alongside of it that the most thickly-peopled,
the noisiest, and in some respects the least repu-
table quarter of Rome lay, called the Suburra.
Descending the Quirinal Hill by the broad
street that leads from the Church of S. Maria
Maggiore, we come to an open square called the
Piazza Barberini, on one side of which is the,
Palazzo Barberini, a vast pile of building without
the slightest architectural beauty. It is now partly
occupied by a squadron of French dragoons, and
Mrs. Story, a well-known American sculptor, has
also her studio there. Its chief interest—at all
events its chief interest to me—was that it contained Guido's celebrated picture of Beatrice Cenci,
who was put to death in 1599, on the charge of
having murdered her father to avenge a foul
outrage he had attempted to commit. It is said
that Guido saw her on the way to the scaffold,
and, struck with her exquisite beauty, afterwards
painted the picture from memory. Another story
is that he obtained admission to her prison the
night before her execution, and painted it in her
cell. The real facts of her tragic story are not
known. They exist, I believe, in the archives of
the Vatican, where the records of the trial are

kept buried, for no one has been allowed to have access to them, and this chiefly because they are thought to compromise the character of Pope Clement VIII. with reference to the conduct of the trial, and to show how unjustly he behaved in refusing to listen to the urgent appeals made to him to save the prisoner's life. I think that no one can gaze on the bewitching beauty of that sweet child-like face, as Guido has painted it, without not only hoping, but believing, that she was innocent.

From the Piazza Barberini the ground ascends, and a long street leads up to the Pincian Hill which runs from the Porta del Popolo, the old Flaminian Gate, by which all travellers coming from the north enter Rome, and extends as far south as the Quirinal, dipping down to it by a street called the Via Gregoriana, the favourite residence of the English during the winter. A zig-zag road leads up to the northern extremity from the Piazza del Popolo, and the top of it at this part is laid out as a public promenade with trees and flowers, which are very appropriate, considering its ancient name, which was Collis Hortulorum, or the Hill of Gardens.

Here it was that Lucullus, the famous epicure

of Rome, had his magnificent house of fabulous cost and splendour. He once asked Cicero and Hortensius to sup with him, and they promised to do so if he would make no special preparation, but consent in fact to let them take "pot luck" with him. He agreed, and turning to one of his slaves merely said, " I will sup to-night in the hall of Apollo." The guests came at the appointed hour, and were astonished to find themselves received at a table of princely profusion. The banquet is said to have cost about 2,800*l*. But in truth the luxury of those old Romans almost surpasses belief. The sums they spent on their fish ponds, and oyster beds, and baths, and suppers, would make modern spendthrifts stand aghast. Even Julius Cæsar used to travel with a set of mosaics to pave the floor of his tent when he halted. Fancy such a thing told of the Duke of Wellington !

Some antiquaries think that at the north end of the Pincian Hill were the gardens of the Domitian family, although others attribute the remains that have been found there to the gardens of Pompey. It is certain that a tomb or sepulchral monument of the Domitian family stood somewhere in this vicinity, as Suetonius expressly mentions that the ashes of Nero were placed there,—and that it stood in the Hill of Gardens, conspicuous from the Campus Martius.

Just below this part of the hill, that is in the Piazza del Popolo, between the gate and the road leading up to the top, is the Church of S. Maria del Popolo, which according to tradition occupies the site of the spot were Nero was buried. The story of his death, as given by Tacitus, is worth telling :

When the provinces had declared in favour of Galba, and the empire was in open revolt against his authority, Nero lost all courage, and gave himself up to abject despair. Ever since the murder of his mother by his parricidal hands he had been haunted by terrible dreams. In one of them he fancied himself dragged down into a dark abyss and covered with a black swarm of winged ants At last, when letters were brought to him while at dinner, which announced that the whole of his army had deserted him, he rose in haste, upset the table, and dashed two costly goblets to the ground. He then filled a golden phial with poison, and thought of rushing to the Forum and appealing there to the compassion of the populace. He actually composed a speech for the occasion, which was afterwards found in his desk, but he

did not dare to face the people, for he was, says
the historian, afraid of being torn to pieces. He
rose in terror at midnight, and went to several
houses of his acquaintance, but could gain admission in none. He then returned to his palace,
and called for some one to come and stab him.
Not a soul appeared; and he then uttered that cry
of utter isolation, " Have I then neither a friend
nor an enemy ? " He next rushed out to throw
himself into the Tiber, but his courage failed him ;
and he determined to try and conceal himself in
a small house which belonged to his freedman
Phaon, about four miles from the city on the east
side, between the Salarian and Numentan roads—
a spot which I have passed on horseback. The
trembling Emperor, having put on an old and
shabby cloak, and holding a napkin before his
face, mounted a horse, and with four attendants
hastened to Phaon's villa. As he went his horse
shied at a dead carcase which lay in the road, and
as the napkin dropped from his face he was recog-
nised by one of the Prætorian guards. When he
got near the house he dismounted, and with naked
feet forced his way through a tangled mass of
bushes and reeds up to the wall at a part where
there was no door, and he here hid himself while

an entrance was dug for him, for he did not dare
to show himself at the gate. Phaon suggested
that he should hide himself in one of the sand-
pits or granno—which we know still exist there
converted into catacombs ; but Nero shuddered at
the idea of what he considered a living tomb. He
drank some muddy water and then crawled on all-
fours through the passage they had made under
the wall, and threw himself on a couch covered
with some old straw. Here, when his attendants
urged him to make away with himself, he hesitated
and sobbed, and at last begged them to prepare
the materials for his funeral, exclaiming, " What
an artist is lost in me ! "—*Qualis artifex pereo !*
A messenger of Phaon now arrived from Rome
with the news that the Senate had declared Nero
a public enemy, and demanded that he should be
punished " after the manner of their ancestors."
" What does that mean ? " asked the trembling
Emperor. He was told that it meant being fixed
naked with the neck in a cross piece of wood and
scourged to death. In an agony of terror Nero
now began to feel the edge of two daggers which
he had brought with him, but thrust them into
their sheaths, exclaiming, " The fatal hour has not
yet come." But it had come. At that moment

the galloping of horses was heard, and Nero, who had prided himself on being a poet and an actor, hurriedly repeated the line from Homer—

"The noise of swift-footed steeds strikes my ear ;"

and with trembling hand, which required the assistance of his secretary, he stabbed himself in the throat. The centurion who had been sent to arrest him came up just as he expired, with the words upon his lips—

" Too late! this is your loyalty "—*Sero : hæc est fides.*

The view from the top of the Pincian Hill is very beautiful. You look westward towards St. Peter's and the Vatican on the other side of the Tiber, with modern Rome spread like a map before you. One of the most conspicuous objects in the distance in front is the Castle of S. Angelo, which was originally the mausoleum of the Emperor Hadrian ; and about a furlong from the Pincian Hill, as it rises above the Piazza del Popolo, stand the remains of the only other mausoleum properly so called in Rome, the destiny of which has been very different. It is the mausoleum of Augustus, formerly one of the noblest monuments of the Campus Martius, and surrounded by shady groves

and gardens, but now choked by the surrounding
houses, and so desecrated that it is difficult to find
it. It is used as a sort of Astley's Circus, and
a strolling equestrian troop exhibits its harlequin
performances in the last resting-place of the great

CASTLE OF S. ANGELO.

Julian family, where were deposited the ashes of
Augustus, and Livia, and Marcellus, of Drusus,
and Germanicus, and Agrippinus, and Tiberius,
and Caligula. Not that I mean to insinuate that

any. reverence or respect is due to the tomb of the two last-named monsters. I found one of the sepulchral chambers full of tawdry stage dresses, and another was used as a stable :—

" Quandoquidem data sunt ipsis quoque fata sepulchris."

The first person who was buried there, or rather whose ashes were placed there—for it was the general custom at Rome to burn the bodies of the dead—was the young Marcellus, the nephew of Augustus, and destined heir of his throne, whose premature death at an early age caused the deepest grief, and is touchingly alluded to by Virgil in the well-known passage of the Æneid, where he represents Anchises in Hades foreshadowing to his son Æneas the future destiny of his descendants :

" What groan of men shall fill the Martian field !
 How fierce a blaze his flaming fire shall yield !
 What funeral pomp shall floating Tiber see,
 When rising from his bed he views the sad solemnity ! "

At the southern end of the Pincian Hill there is the Church of S. Trinita dei Monti, the front of which faces due west, and a broad flight of few steps leads up to it from the Piazza di Spagna. These stairs are a favourite haunt of beggars and models. By models I mean men who sit to painters and sculptors, and who come here to attract notice and be hired. Dickens thus speaks of these stairs in his amusing "Pictures from Italy":— " There is one old gentleman with long white hair and an immense beard, who to my knowledge has gone half through the catalogue of the Royal Academy. This is the venerable or patriarchal model. He carries a long staff, and every knot and twist in that staff I have seen faithfully delineated innumerable times. There is another man in a blue cloak, who always pretends to be asleep in the sun (when there is any), and who I need not say is always very wide awake, and very attentive to the disposition of his legs. This is the *dolce far niente* model. There is another man in a brown cloak, who leans against a wall with his arms folded in his mantle, and looks out of the corners of his eyes, which are just visible beneath his broad slouched hat. This is the assassin model. There is another man who constantly looks over his own shoulder, and is always going away but never goes. This is the haughty or scornful model."

As to the beggars, they are always to be found there, and that it is a lucrative locality for them I think the following anecdote will show :—When I was in Rome a beggar used to take his stand on these steps, whose daughter had been lately married, and to whom he was able to give a very handsome sum of money by way of dowry. A gentleman who had heard of this one day accosted the beggar at his usual post, and asked him how he had the face to solicit alms when it was notorious that he had had the means of settling a small fortune on his daughter; to which the old rascal replied, " O yes, this is very true, I did give her a portion, but I have now got another daughter to marry." And so he continues, if he is still alive, to levy contributions on the public for that laudable object.

The number of beggars in the streets is a disgrace to Rome. I never saw anything like it elsewhere in my life—except perhaps in going up a hill in France in the old days of diligences, when you were sure to be assailed by a cry of " *pauvre miserable* " from a crowd of mendicants, who looked upon every traveller as a prey specially destined by Providence for their support. And perhaps I ought also to except at the present day the few miles of road between Bayonne and Biarritz, where there is no hill, but where the beggars literally swarm, or at least did so when I was there in 1855. I remember one old gentleman

riding up to me on his donkey, and taking off his
hat to me, a courtesy which I returned, and it was
some time before I could believe that he was
begging me to give him a sous. At Rome a stiff
joint or a wounded finger—not to speak of any
form of loathsome disease—is a capital stock in
trade, and the fortunate possessor turns it to good
account. Even the priests beg. Of course I do
not mean any of the respectable secular clergy,
but some of the monks, who are truly mendicant
friars; and I used frequently to have a tin money-
box politely offered to my notice by one of the
fraternity of a convent sent out to collect alms.
I must, however, do the Roman beggars the justice
to say they are not often importunate, and if
refused they are never impudent. They ply their
trade from morning to night, and of course cannot
expect that all passers-by will be soft enough to
respond to their appeal. They therefore quietly
pocket not the money but the affront, and immediately look out for the next comer.

As however we have been led to speak of the
streets of Rome, let us now descend into them,
and take a ramble through them, confining our
attention to some of the most remarkable objects.
The best point to start from, and that which will

give the most accurate idea of the plan and con-
figuration of the city, is the Piazza del Popolo, the
open square at the extreme north, into which you
enter from the *Porta del Popolo*, the old Flaminian
Gate. From this place three streets radiate, which
are three of the main arteries of Rome. The one
on the right is the Via Ripetta, which runs parallel
and close to the Tiber, but is separated from it by
the row of houses which lines the street. About
half-way down the Ripetta there is a ferry called
Porto di Ripetta across the Tiber, and on the
other side were the meadows of Quinctius (*prata
Quinctia*) where Cincinnatus was living in a small
cottage and cultivating the cabbages, when, according to the story, he was summoned by a deputation
from the Senate to be Dictator of Rome. The
street in the middle is the Corso, the chief street in
Rome, which leads past the Capitol straight to the
Forum, about a mile and a half distant. The one on
the left is the Via di Babuino, which runs along the
base of the Pincian Hill, and leads into the Piazza
di Spagna. The space between the Ripetta and the
Babuino—that is, in fact, almost the whole space
from the Piazza del Popolo to the Capitol—forms an
irregular triangle, and was the old Campus Martius,
through the centre of which the Corso runs, and on

which almost the whole—or at all events by far the greatest part—of modern Rome is built. Cicero mentions that in his time there was a talk of diverting the bed of the Tiber at the Milvian bridge, and making it flow more to the westward under the Vatican Hill, so as to unite the Campus Vaticanus with the Campus Martius, which it divides from it. The object of this was to make use of the Campus Martius as building ground, and so increase the size of the city, while the Campus Vaticanus would remain open, and so serve the purpose of the Campus Martius; but the project was never realized.

The walls of Rome however embrace a much wider circuit, but between them and the part I have just described there are vast tracts of ground unoccupied by buildings except ruins, such as the Baths of Caracalla, and Diocletian, and Titus, or broken aqueducts like that of Claudius, or remains of gardens like those of Sallust. You may wander a long summer's day in this desolate region, threading on foot or on horseback the long narrow lanes which divided the vineyards ;—and ruins, such as I have mentioned, with here and there a solitary church, are all you will meet with in the intramural space to the east and south of the streets of

G 2

the existing city. To me, I confess, there was an inexpressible charm in this part of Rome. Here was the dwelling-place of the ancient mistress of the world—and here fitting silence brooded over the space no longer tenanted by man and haunted by the memories of the past.

Starting now from Piazza del Popolo let us walk down the Corso—the longest, straightest, and most important street in Rome. The shops however are very disappointing. They will not stand a comparison in size or building with those of Regent Street in London or the Rue de la Paix in Paris, nor in fact with those of many provincial towns in England and France. They have a dingy and rather melancholy look, and there is an entire absence of anything like activity and bustle about them. The first striking building we come to is one on the right hand. It is an old palace, the Palazzo Ruspoli, the ground floor of which is converted into a café—called the Café Nuovo. In its gloom and silence it is an apt representation of the Cave of Trophonius. Beyond this, on the same side, is an open piazza called Piazza de Colonna, where stands the noble column of Antonine. It was erected by the Senate and people in honour of Marcus Aurelius A.D. 174, and is sculptured with

THE PANTHEON,

bas-reliefs running round it in a spiral form, which
represent contests with and victories over barbarian
tribes.

. If we go across this piazza and then thread our
way through the streets beyond it, towards the left,
we shall come to the Piazza di Rotonda, one side
of which is occupied by the most perfect relic of
ancient Rome, the Pantheon. It is a circular building of uncased Roman brick, with a fine portico in
front, and a dome which was formerly covered
with bronze. It was erected by Agrippa in his
third consulate, B.C. 27. Byron calls it

> " Sanctuary and home
> Of art and piety—Pantheon, pride of Rome !"

and Forsyth, in his " Italy," says of its portico that
it is " more than faultless ; it is positively the most
sublime result that was ever produced by so little
architecture." It was converted in the seventh
century into a Christian church ; and here in the
sixteenth Raphael, the king of painters, was buried.
Until a few years ago it was supposed, for what
reason I know not, that a skull kept in the
Academy of St. Luke, one of the picture galleries
in Rome, was his ; but in 1833 his coffin in the
Pantheon was opened, and there, as might. be

expected, the real head was found. A friend of mine told me that he saw the body, which was exhibited for some days under a glass case, and it had much the appearance of an Egyptian mummy.

I do not know the reason why, but I never passed across the piazza of the Pantheon without seeing there owls or rather owlets for sale. They are kept perched on the ends of long sticks, to which they are fastened by the leg, and it is very absurd to see them in the middle of the day blinking in the sunshine and looking very uncomfortable. One would have thought a more appropriate place for them would be the Piazza di Minerva, which is a short distance behind the Pantheon, for the owl was the bird dedicated to Minerva, and hence supposed to be the symbol of wisdom. But we are wandering too far from the Corso, and must return to the place where we left it, namely, the Piazza di Colonna. There are several palaces of the Roman nobility which line the sides of the Corso as we walk southwards, but the most striking and the most richly furnished, and the one which contains the most valuable gallery of pictures, is the Palazzo Doria. It contains some fine paintings, amongst which I may mention the Sacrifice of Isaac, by Titian; a portrait of Joanna II. of

Aragon, Queen of Naples, by Leonardo da Vinci ; a Magdalene, by Annibali Caracci; and some beautiful landscapes by Claude.

Just beyond this we come to a point where the Corso properly so called ends, and in order to proceed onwards to the Forum we must go along a narrower street called the Via di Marforio. It is made up of two words, *Martis* and *Forum*, and indicates that here formerly stood the Temple of Mars close by the Forum of Augustus, for he gave Rome a forum in addition to those previously existing. At the commencement of the *Via di Marforio*, and forming part of or rather built into the wall of a house on the left hand, is a curious and interesting relic of the days of Republican Rome. It is the remains of the tomb of Bibulus, and an inscription still legible informs us that it was given to him as "a mark of honour on account of his virtue by a decree of the Senate and the command of the people—" SENATUS CONSULTO POPULIQUE JUSSU HONORIS VIRTUTISQUE CAUSA." It stands on a spot which is supposed to have been just outside of the gate, in the old wall of Servius Tullius, called Porta Ratumena ; all traces of which have now entirely disappeared. And the reason why antiquaries place it outside the walls is

because by a law of the Twelve Tables no one was
allowed to be buried within them—"HOMINEM
MORTUUM IN URBE NE SEPELITO NEVE URITO." But
this is not conclusive, for Cicero expressly mentions (de Legg. II. 20) that an exception was
sometimes made in the case of distinguished merit
(*virtutis causâ*), which was exactly what may have
happened with respect to Bibulus.

The existing walls were not built until several
centuries after he had become the occupant of his
honourable tomb. I ought to have mentioned that
just before you reach the *Via di Marforio* there
stands, on the right hand, a building of such an
enormous size that it must arrest every stranger's
attention, and make him ask, as I did, its name
and purpose. I saw it first at night, and it
happened at that particular time to be illuminated
by countless wax candles, so that the effect was
very striking. I applied to a priest who was
standing by me for information, and he told me
that this was the Palazzo de Venezia, and *le plus
beau point de Rome*. It was sold in the sixteenth
century by Pope Clement VIII. to Venice, and
hence its name; but on the downfall of the Republic it passed to the Emperor of Austria; and
the reason of the illumination I saw was that it

was the day dedicated to the patron saint of the Emperor, which of course occurs only once a year. If we turn to the left just after passing the tomb of Bibulus, and go up a short street, we come to the Foro Trajano or Trajan's Forum, part of which has been recently excavated, and it is a very interesting spot. It is a large oblong space, the centre of which is occupied by so much of the ancient forum as has been laid bare, the bottom of it being about ten feet lower than the surrounding streets. At the north end stands the noble column of Trajan, one of the finest objects in Rome, and in front of this, to the south, is the excavated site of part of a large basilica called the Basilica Ulfia, from the family name of Trajan, as I have already mentioned. Gibbon, the historian, speaking of the Forum of Trajan, says, "It was surrounded with a lofty portico in the form of a quadrangle, into which four triumphal arches opened a noble and spacious entrance: in the centre arose a column of marble whose height of one hundred and ten feet denoted the elevation of the hill that had been cut away."* I have already mentioned that the hill thus divided was the ridge of which the two extremities were called the Capitoline and Quirinal

* Decline and Fall, i. 2.

Hills. The connexion between which was continuous until Trajan cut them in two by making his forum.

One of the most interesting excursions that can be made at Rome is to visit the Via Appia, or Street of Tombs, that runs in a straight line, due south, from the Porta S. Sebastiano (formerly the Porta Appia) as far as Albano, a distance of about fourteen miles. It derives its name from Appius Claudius Cæcus, the Censor, by whom it was commenced at the end of the fourth century before Christ. When completed as far as Brundusium on the coast it became the great line of communication between Rome and Southern Italy; and is well described by Statius, one of the later Latin poets, as REGINA VIARUM, or THE QUEEN OF WAYS.* It began originally at a point where the old Porta Capena or Capuan Gate stood, nearly a mile within the existing wall—for I may mention in passing that the old wall of Servius Tullius, in which the Porta Capena was one of the gates, circumscribed a much smaller area than the wall of Aurelius, which became afterwards the boundary of the city, and is still perfect. Until, however, we reach the Porta S. Sebastiano the appearance of the road is

* " Appia longarum teritur Regina Viarum."

APPIAN WAY.

modern, it being in fact overlaid by later material, and there is nothing to distinguish its construction, or *metalling*, as I believe it is technically called, from the other roads in the neighbourhood. But before we reach the gate there are one or two objects of interest on which I will say a few words. On our right hand, about a furlong off the road, stand the colossal ruins of the Baths of Caracalla. These and the remains of the Baths of Diocletian and the Baths of Titus strike every beholder with astonishment. They were on a scale of grandeur and magnificence of which it is difficult for us to form an idea. Those of Caracalla occupied a space of nearly a mile in circuit and would accommodate 1,600 bathers at a time; and this was only half the size of the Baths of Diocletian, which could accommodate 3,200 bathers. But, as has been re- marked, " the Thermæ, or Baths, properly speaking, were a Roman adaptation of the Greek gymnasium or palæstra, both of which contained a system of baths in conjunction with conveniences for athletic games and youthful sports, *exhedræ* in which the rhetoricians declaimed, poets recited, and philoso- phers lectured, as well as porticoes and vestibules for the idle, and libraries for the learned. They were decorated with the finest objects of art, both in painting and sculpture, covered with precious marbles, and adorned with fountains and shaded walks, and plantations like the groves of the Academy."* I should only fatigue you by attempt_

BATHS OF CARACALLA.

ing to describe the interior arrangements of these enormous buildings, upon which a profusion of learning has been lavished by scholars. All there is ruin now. Shelley says, in his preface to 'Prometheus Unbound,' "This poem was chiefly written

* Smith's " Dictionary of Greek and Roman Antiquities."

upon the mountainous ruins of the Baths of Caracalla, among the flowery glades and thickets of odoriferous blossoming trees, which are extended in ever winding labyrinths upon its immense platforms, and dizzy arches suspended in the air."

Leaving these ruins we now proceed towards the Porta S. Sebastiano, and meet with some very interesting sepulchral monuments in the space between the site of the old Capena and the existing gate. There is the tomb of the Scipios, and there are the columbaria in a vineyard on the left hand as we approach close to the walls.

I rang a bell at a door in the garden wall, and it was opened by an old woman who shows the tomb. At the end of a short pathway from the door we saw what looked exactly like the entrance of a cave on the site of some rising ground. Here we lighted tapers; and, entering a dark passage, found ourselves in the burying-place of the great Cornelian family of the Scipios. It consists of several subterranean chambers, where the sarcophagi or stone coffins once rested, but are no longer to be found there.

The Scipios' tomb contains no ashes now, for they have been removed to various museums; the most celebrated being that of which there are

many models sold in the shops. It is the sarcophagus in *peperino* stone, in which lay the ashes
of Lucius Scipio Barbatus, and which is now in
the Vatican. Of all the monuments of ancient
Rome this is the one which is more frequently
produced in miniature in marble or bronze
than any other, except perhaps the Temple of
Vesta.

Not far from the Scipios' tomb, and in the same
straggling vineyard, are two of those curious bury-
ing-places called "*columbaria*," of which several
have within the last few years been discovered.
They might properly be called burying-*pits*, for
they are sunk deep into the ground, and you descend into them by a flight of ancient steps. They
are of a square or oblong shape, and the sides are
entirely filled with rows of little niches containing
the urns : some in bronze, and some in marble or
terra cotta, in which the ashes of the dead were
deposited after the corpse had been burnt on the
funeral pyre. These niches are not unlike the
holes of pigeon-houses, and hence the name of
columbaria has been given to them ; but I believe
it does not occur in any classic author, and is
only found in one ancient inscription. I should
think that the depth of the two that I explored

was about fifteen feet, and they were sheltered
with roofs, which are, however, quite modern, for
when the pits were discovered they were filled
with earth, which has been carefully excavated.
Under each niche is an inscription with the name
of the deceased, and sometimes an affecting senti-
ment. . I remember one, which reminded me of
the curse attributed to Shakespeare against any
one who should remove his bones, for it denounced
the vengeance of the infernal gods upon the head
of whoever disturbed the ashes resting there.
Close to the columbaria is a cottage, where the
keeper of them has a large collection of antiquities,
dug up in the neighbourhood or elsewhere : such
as signet rings, cameos, bronze figures and im-
plements, cresset lamps, and such like curiosities.
And here I may mention a mistake which is
generally made with regard to the little glass
bottles which are frequently found in funeral urns,
and which have been called lachrymatories, from
the idea that they were tear bottles, intended, I
suppose, to be emblematic of the sorrow felt for
the death of the departed. But they were in
reality what we should now call scent bottles, that
is, little flasks filled with a few drops of the per-
fumed oil or spirit, which was poured over the

ashes of the corpse after it had been consumed by fire.

When we pass through the Porta S. Sebastiano we see at once that we are upon the ancient road. It has been cleared out, and the old foundation in many parts laid bare during the reign of the present Pope, under the able superintendence of the late Commendatore Jacobini, who was Minister of Public Works and Fine Arts. It is not, however, till we nearly reach the Tomb of Cæcilia Metella, about two miles farther on, that we see the old polygonal slabs of stone which are the characteristic sign of a Roman road. A few yards beyond the Sebastian Gate was found the first milestone of the Via Appia, which commenced, as you will remember, at the Porta Capena, nearly a mile inside the existing wall; and this milestone now stands on the balustrade at the top of the steps leading up to the north side of the Capitol.

I do not propose to notice in detail the various objects of interest that lie on each side of the road as we proceed, such as the ruins of the so-called sepulchre of Geta, who was, with his brother Caracalla, joint Emperor of Rome ; the Church of *Domine quo vades?* where, according to the old

tradition, St. Peter met our Saviour and asked
Him, " Lord, whither goest Thou?"; the shady grove
of trees, where, contrary to all good authority, I
believe, the local guides place the Fountain of
Egeria, that mysterious nymph to whom Numa
Pompilius, the Roman king, paid secret nocturnal
visits;* the ruins of the Temple of Romulus, I do
not mean the founder of Rome, but Romulus the
son of the Emperor Maxentius, and of the Circus
of Romulus or Maxentius, which was built in
honour of that Romulus at the beginning of the
fourth century after Christ. I wandered about the
circus, a scene of lonely desolation, for some time
on a lovely day. It is of oblong shape, and surrounded by the old ruined wall, on the inside of
which were the seats for the spectators ; and the
arena, which is covered with grass and flowers,
would make an excellent racecourse now—being
quite long enough, although perhaps rather narrow
at what we should call the bend for horses going

* It is certain that the Roman authors placed the fountain of
Egeria in a different spot, namely, in the low ground between
the Porta Capena and the Porta Appia. Thus Juvenal says,
Sat. III.—
    " Substitit ad veteres arcus madidamque Capenam.
    Hic, ubi nocturnæ Numa constituebat amicæ.
    Nunc sacri fontis nemus et delubra locantur
    Judæis."

H

round it at full speed. It lies to the left of the
Appian Way, and the Tomb of Cæcilia Metella
on the same side of the road, and just immediately
beyond it. It was erected B.C. 67 to the memory
of Cæcilia, the daughter of Quintus Metellus, the
conqueror of Crete, and wife of Crassus, as a simple
inscription on a marble slab in the wall informs
us. It consists of a circular tower resting on a
square basement, and is of the most massive construction, and of enormous strength.* During the
Middle Ages it was, like many other of the old
monuments, converted into a feudal stronghold;
but it sustained most injury when the Constable
Bourbon besieged Rome in 1527. The interior is
now empty, and no one knows what has become
of the sarcophagus that contained the body of her
for whom this magnificent mausoleum was built.
I saw one standing in the Court of the Farnese
Palace, which is supposed to have been found in
it; but in Murray's "Handbook" this is said to be
on doubtful authority.

I did not go more than a furlong beyond Cæcilia
Metella's tomb along the Appian Way, but I saw

---

* " There is a stern round tower of other days
Firm as a fortress," &c.
                          CHILDE HAROLD, Canto IV.

TOMB OF CÆCILIA METELLA. Page 114.

it stretching before me in a straight line right across the Campagna, as far as Albano, its course being marked by dotted heaps of stone, the ruins of tombs, and temples, and villas, and *exhedræ*, or resting-places for weary travellers. Amazing, indeed, is the contrast between this part of the Campagna and what it was in the days of the Empire. The silent and deserted track that now threads its way through the desolate plain was then a busy highway, thronged with passengers, and lined with stately buildings. To realize the scene we may avail ourselves of Milton's description—

> " Thence to the gates cast round thine eye, and see
> What conflux issuing forth, or entering in ;
> Prætors, proconsuls to their provinces
> Hasting, or on return, in robes of state ;
> Lictors and rods, the ensigns of their power,
> Legions and cohorts, turms of horse and wings :
> Or embassies from regions far remote
> In various habits on the Appian road."

To our notions, indeed, the sight of so many sepulchres must have had rather a lugubrious effect, but the Romans do not seem to have thought so. They had some odd notions with respect to the interment of the dead, and even Merry-Andrews attended their funerals. The sides of the road were here and there enlivened by gay villas and beautiful temples, and some of the emperors had country houses here. The ruins of that of Gallienus may still be seen near where stood the ninth milestone, and it was amongst them that the statue of the Discobolus, or Quoit-thrower, which is now in the Vatican, was dis-covered in the last century.

There are still a few farms scattered over the Campagna in this direction, and at the point where I stopped a large field was being ploughed by oxen. But it is so unhealthy that it is a marvel that any persons venture to live there, and I cannot give you a better idea of what is now thought of its melancholy state than by men-tioning a story that was told me at Rome of a young artist who, having been overtaken by night-fall when sketching in the Campagna, was torn to pieces by wild dogs. I was told also that some time ago a proposal had been made to form a company by some English or German (I forget which) and Belgian speculators, for the purpose of reclaiming and colonizing the district, but the Papal Government refused to give its consent to the scheme.

I have purposely omitted to mention two most

interesting objects which we have passed on our
way to Cæcilia Metella's tomb. These are the
catacombs of S. Callixtus and S. Sebastian, both
which lie on the right hand, and at a short distance from each other. Their history and asso-
ciations are exclusively Christian, or perhaps,
rather, they are the silent memorials of the
struggle between Christianity and Paganism, and
I have therefore reserved them for a separate
mention by themselves. But the subject of the
catacombs is so large, and has been so elaborately
investigated by Bosio, Marchi and Perret amongst
foreign writers, and by Dr. Maitland, not to mention Macfarlane and Northcote, amongst our own,
that it would be idle for me to attempt to give
even the faintest outline of their researches in the
limits to which I am confined. I will merely
mention a few leading and interesting facts, and
then describe what I actually saw.

Under the Campagna, in various directions in
the neighbourhood of Rome, and even under some
parts within the walls, the ground is honeycombed
in an extraordinary manner by subterranean passages cut in the soft *tufa*, or *puzzalano* soil, which
when exposed to the air soon hardens, and is the
chief material out of which the buildings at Rome

have been constructed. They are supposed to have been very ancient quarries—much older than Rome itself, and they were called by the Romans *arenaria*, or sand-pits. They are found not only at Rome, but at Naples, in Sicily, in Greece, and in Asia Minor, in the vicinity of which were even larger towns. These were made use of by the Romans for building, and new ones were opened by them as the old became exhausted, until at length they extended for many miles, like the narrow streets of a buried city. Some of them appear to have been afterwards used as cemeteries for the poor, for, as I have already mentioned, the Esquiline caverns were, according to Horace, " the common sepulchre of the miserable plebeians," whose bodies were interred, and not burnt, as was the case with the richer classes of society. They also were the haunts of robbers and banditti, and Cicero mentions in one of his orations (*pro Cluentio*) that Asinius, a young citizen of Rome, was decoyed on some pretext out of the city, and dragged into the quarries or sand-pits near the Esquiline Gate, where he was murdered. In fact, they became what until lately the ruins of the Colosseum were—the resort of assassins and other bad characters, from the

facility they afforded for deeds of villany, and
also for escape. When Nero was trembling for
his life he was advised by his freedman, Phaon,
to take refuge in one of the three subterranean
quarries, but he declared that he could not consent
to bury himself alive. It may easily be imagined
that when the Christians became sufficiently numerous at Rome to attract the attention of the
authorities, and were exposed to injury and insult,
they bethought themselves of these crypts or
hiding-places from their oppressors, where they
would be able to celebrate their religious rites un-
observed ; and the long passages in a soil which
was so easily excavated, furnished them with easy
and convenient receptacles for their dead, whom
of course they always buried, and never burnt,
animated by the hope of a joyful resurrection
when "this corruption shall inherit incorruption,
and this mortal put on immortality." I need not
speak of the cruel and bloody persecution of the
Christians under Nero, and Domitian, and Trajan,
and Severus, and Maximus, and Decius, and Diocletian, which would have destroyed any religion
other than divine; but it is obvious how, when
once the early Christians found an asylum underground, where they were comparatively safe, they

must have flocked there in crowds during the storm that raged against them. The old galleries of the quarries became at once the sepulchres of the dead and the abodes of the living. This short account will sufficiently explain the origin and use of the catacombs, a name of doubtful origin, which seems to have been at first applied only to

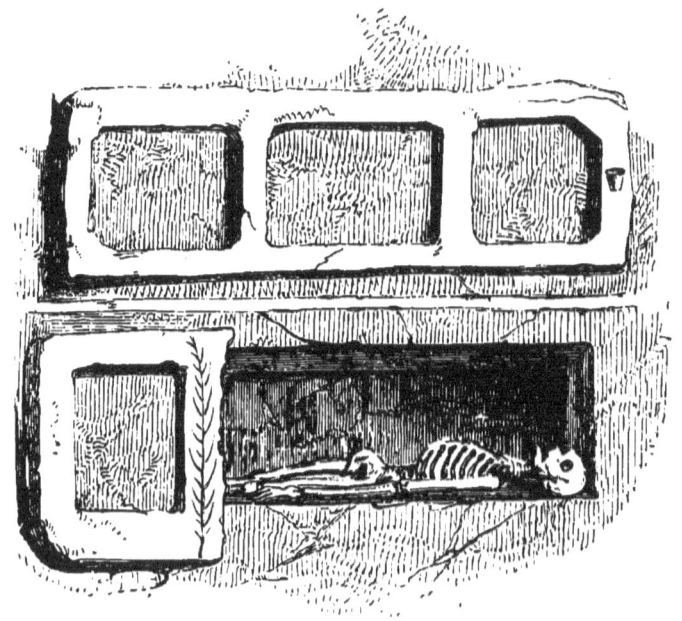

THE CATACOMBS.

the Church of S. Sebastian, where according to tradition the bodies of St. Peter and St. Paul were for a time deposited.*

* The word "catacombs" is supposed to be derived from

The Church of S. Sebastian, where you descend into that part of the catacombs that lies in the immediate neighbourhood, is a little off the road on the right hand going from Rome. We found a monk there ready to act as our guide, and having lighted candles at the lamp, which is kept burning before an image of the Virgin, we followed him into a side chamber, where there was a yawning and dark opening, into which we went, as if about to plunge into a cellar. We soon got into a narrow subterranean passage, and went twisting about until I felt perfectly certain that if I were left alone there, even with a light, I should have the greatest possible difficulty in finding my way out again, and of course in the dark it would be utterly hopeless. We saw on each side of the passage an immense number of empty receptacles for dead bodies, but all the monuments and stone coffins had been removed to the Vatican, except, I think, one or two slabs, the inscriptions on which indicated that martyrs had been buried there, and if I remember rightly one of these was the stone on which the decapitation had actually taken place, although of course not at that spot.

two Greek words κατὰ κύμβη. The earliest mention of the word occurs in a letter to Pope Gregory the Great at the end of the sixth century, who speaks of *locus qui dicitur catacombus*.

It is difficult to understand how the fugitive Christians could live in these dark recesses, and I do not believe it would have been possible to do so in those which I visited; but there are other catacombs much more extensive which I had not time to explore; the principal are those of S. Calixtus, not far from the Church of S. Sebastian, and those of S. Agnese, a church and convent on the Via Pia, to the east of Rome, and about a mile outside the walls.

There is an immense collection of the stone monuments and inscriptions taken from the catacombs in the Vatican, and most interesting they are. Most of the epitaphs have a touching simplicity, which contrasts strongly with the pompous and laboured eulogiums that distinguish modern monuments. Such for instance are the following :

" Arethusa dormit in Deo."
Arethusa sleeps in God.

" Lavinia melle dulcior quiescit in pace."
Lavinia, sweeter than honey, rests in peace.

" Juliæ innocenti et dulci mater sua sperans."
To Julia, the innocent and sweet, her mother in hope.

" Vitellianus magister militum quiescit in Domino Jesu."
Vitellianus a military captain rests in the Lord Jesus.

But I must not linger on this interesting subject ;

and as we are now outside the walls of Rome, I
propose that we should make an excursion to
Tusculum, which lies about fourteen miles to
the east of Rome. We can get there without
any difficulty as there is a railway across the
Campagna, which divides into two at a place called
Stazione di Campagna, one fork or branch leading to Frascati, below Tusculum, and the other
to Albano. The railway station is just outside the
S. Lorenz Gate. The carriages are very com-
fortable, and the locomotive is very good, being
an importation from England, as you may see by
the names of the manufacturers upon it. Frascati
is beautifully situated on the slope of the mountains to the east of Rome, which sparkle with
the villas of the Roman nobility, who resort to
them for the summer and autumn months, and
the terminus of the railway is on the plain about
a mile below. The site of the ancient city of
Tusculum is two miles above Frascati, and a
lovelier walk can hardly be imagined. The path
leads, with a continuous ascent, through woods
and past villas and convents, " bosomed high in
tufted trees," until we strike into a narrow lane,
paved with ancient blocks of flat stone, which is
the actual *Clivus Tusculi*, or old road, up which no

doubt Cicero often walked or was carried in a litter according to the Roman fashion, as he went to his favourite Tusculan villa, where he wrote some of his most celebrated philosophical works. Passing this lane we reach a romantic spot, where are the remains of a small amphitheatre, which need not detain us; and a little further on to the right, on a grassy platform jutting out on the south-west side of the hill, and commanding a most exquisite view, is the site of Cicero's villa called Tusculanum. Antiquaries, indeed, who throw doubt upon everything, tell you that there is no certainty that this *is* the site, and some call it the villa of Tiberius. But very possibly that emperor may afterwards have been the owner of the villa that once was Cicero's, just as Scylla was before Cicero bought it. And I see no reason to doubt that on this very spot stood the favourite residence of the great Roman orator. He had a peculiar affection for the place, and it would not be easy to find a more charming situation. In his letter to Atticus he frequently reminds his friend, who was then at Athens, to send him pictures and statues to ornament his villa, and mentions that he had built there an academy in imitation of the one at Athens, and also a gymnasium. Just above the villa there is a small cottage, like what we should call a forester's lodge, in the walls of which are numerous fragments of statues and inscriptions. And at the corner facing the villa there stands, curiously enough, a tolerably perfect statue of a Roman orator, the attitude being the same as that of the figure so called in the Uffizzi Gallery at Florence.

It was for the sake of Cicero's villa that I made the pilgrimage to Tusculum, and I was amply repaid by what I saw. It so happened that excavations were at that moment going on at the expense of the Aldobrandini family, to whom the property belongs, and I saw chambers and pavements which had been just disinterred from their sleep of ages, and was allowed to carry away some relics which had been dug up that morning. It is supposed that a villa of Tiberius afterwards occupied the site of Cicero's, and this may have been so ; but at all events what I saw were the genuine chambers of an ancient Roman house, with the walls as perfect as when they were first constructed. They were being excavated chiefly on the side of the slope, so that the earth overhead formed a roof, and the walls were lined with small lozenge-shaped pieces of stone known as the *opus vermiculatum* of the ancients. A tremendous

thunder-storm burst over the Campagna while I
was busy in exploring the ruins, and I was glad
to find shelter in these ancient rooms, where I was
as completely protected from the rain as if I had
been in a modern house. They are of small size,
and seem to have been in stories—at all events I
descended into one which was much lower than
the rest. I have no doubt that some interesting
discoveries will be made here if the excavations
are continued. One solitary labourer was alone
employed at the work when I was there, and a
more silent secluded spot can hardly be imagined.

A little higher up the hill is one of the most
perfect specimens of a Roman day theatre, that is
one open to the sky—that exists anywhere. There
it is, after the lapse of 2,000 years, so perfect that,
with the aid of a spade to clear away the earth
that in some parts has overgrown it, you might in
a few hours use it as easily as the good people of
Tusculum did, when they flocked there to see
actors from Rome perform on provincial boards
(that is *stones*) the plays of Plautus and Terence.
Grass and flowers grow upon the stage, and cover .
in wild profusion the semicircular rows of seats,
but hardly a stone seems to be out of its place;
and in this respect, although on quite a miniature

THEATRE TUSCULUM.　　　　　Page 126.

scale, it is better off than any of the remains of the great theatres of Rome. Directly above it rises the beetling top of the hill on which once stood the *arx* or citadel of Tusculum. But where are the remains of Tusculum itself—that ancient city which once was able to cope with Rome in her infancy? They have utterly perished, and were it not for the theatre, and the ruins of the amphitheatre and villa which I have described, it would be difficult to believe that in those wooded solitudes there was once a busy and populous town. It was strong enough to resist the attack of Hannibal in the second Punic war, and it existed almost entire until the end of the twelfth century, when it was utterly destroyed by the Romans to avenge a bloody defeat they had sustained there in 1167, during the contest between the Guelphs and Ghibelines, that is between the Papal and Imperial factions, which so long distracted and devastated Italy.

Hitherto we have been chiefly considering the movements of Pagan Rome; but we must not forget that she was not only the mistress of the ancient world, the

> " Great and glorious Rome, Queen of the Earth
> So far renowned, and with the spoils enriched
> Of nations,"

but at a later period the head of Christendom and
the great repository of art. Before I conclude, therefore, I ought to say a few words about the Eternal
City in reference to these points of view.

I need not say that churches abound at Rome.
A volume might be devoted to them ; and it would
of course be impossible for me here even to glance
at them in the limits within which I must confine
myself. They have all something of interest
attached to them, either in their history, their
architecture, their paintings, their sculptures, or
their legends. But, with hardly an exception,
their exteriors are mean and in bad taste, giving
no promise of the beauty which is so often found
within. Even the most gorgeously furnished of
all except St. Peter's, and the one most recently
built—indeed not yet quite finished (I mean that
of S. Paolo fuori i Muri), though vast in size, has
externally a very ugly look, and in a more indus-
trious country might be taken for a factory. I
must however hasten on to say a few words on *the*
great church of Rome—the largest and noblest in
the world.

In order to reach St. Peter's we must cross the
Tiber by the S. Angelo Bridge, at the opposite end
of which, that is on the right bank of the river,

stands the Castle of S. Angelo, formerly the mausoleum of Hadrian, but now a fortress, occupied
by French troops. It is circular in shape and of
immense strength. A covered gallery runs from it
to the Vatican, a distance of about a third of a
mile ; so that in case of a sudden attack the Pope
would be able to escape from his palace and take
refuge in the castle. Immediately on crossing the
bridge we turn sharp to the left, and go up a street
which leads direct to St. Peter's. At the end of
the street is the Piazza di San Pietro, with the
cathedral in front, and two long colonnades branch-
ing from it in a graceful curve on each side. In
the centre of the square is an Egyptian obelisk*
which formerly stood in the Circus of Caligula,
and two large fountains are also conspicuous
features. The Vatican is on the right as you

---

* The obelisks are a remarkable feature amongst the antiquities at Rome. There were six large ones, two in the Circus
Maximus, one in the Vatican, one in the Campus Martius, and
two in the Mausoleum of Augustus. These all exist now in
different parts of Rome, having been, when found broken, carefully restored by the Popes. They were brought from Egypt by
the Emperors, and generally dedicated to the sun. An inscription upon each records that the Pope who erected it had purified
it from the service of an unholy religion, and dedicated it to the
Virgin or to the glory of God. Besides these there are six others
of smaller size in different localities.

I

approach, and it seems to grow out of St. Peter's like a huge excrescence.

It is an ugly building, but its vast size gives it an imposing look. By far the most favourable view I had of it was while I was riding towards

ST. PETER'S.

it outside the walls along the road that enters Rome by the Porta Angelica. It occupies the north-western extremity of the city wall, which here runs along the edge of a rather steep escarpment of the Monti Vatican or Vatican Hill.

Contrary to what we should expect in the
mother and queen of all churches, the principal
front and entrance of St. Peter's faces the east,
and the altar and chancel are on the west. But
this is by no means peculiar to the cathedral. It
is a common feature of the churches of Rome,
where we find the points of the compass dis-
regarded, and the chancel is placed with as little
reference to the east as if it belonged to a dissent-
ing meeting-house. But this is easily explained
when we bear in mind what I have already said
about the origin of the form of the early Christian
churches. The altar was placed in the tribune of
the basilica, and it was a pure matter of accident
whether the tribune of a law court stood north,
south, east or west.

A succession of very broad flights of steps
occupying the space between the colonnades leads
up to the doors of the church, and I was struck
by the quantity of short grass which I saw growing
there. There really was in front of St. Peter's
enough to form a respectable day's food for a horse
or a cow; and I could not help thinking that this
told a silent tale as regards the number of
worshippers who frequent the church, and this
was confirmed by what I heard at Rome. Except
on a few great occasions, the attendance at St.

Peter's even on Sundays is scanty, and on a week-
day I can bear witness that you may often not
find half a dozen persons there at the same time.
Before we enter let me remind you that the
building as we now see it was erected in the 16th
century, and that Raphael and Michael Angelo,
two of the greatest painters that ever lived, were
amongst its principal architects. The first stone of
St. Peter's, as it now exists, was laid by Pope Julius
II. on the 18th April, 1506, and Bramante was
originally the sole architect. At his death in 1514
Raffaello d'Urbano, the great painter, was appointed
architect, with two associates, by Leo X. When
Raffaello died in 1520 Sanfallo succeeded him,
and on his death, in 1546, Michael Angelo became,
at the request of Paul III. the sole architect. The
magnificent cupola is entirely his work. Indeed
the origin of the building is due to Michael
Angelo, for it arose out of his plan of a mausoleum
for Julius II. which he designed in the lifetime of
that pope, but it never advanced farther than the
design. The celebrated statue of Moses, with
horns and a flowing beard, by Michael Angelo, in
the Church of S. Pietro i Vincoli, was executed by
him for the intended sepulchral monument. The
reason of its non-completion involves a tedious
history, and perhaps cannot be very satisfactorily

explained. But it occupies the site of a much older church, and that again was formed out of a pagan basilica that stood on the same spot. I saw in the Vatican a picture of the ancient church; and there is another which represents the raising the Egyptian obelisk on the piazza, and on which a portion of the former church then in the course of demolition appears.

The façade or front is I think wholly unworthy of the rest of this magnificent temple. It is heavy in appearance, and wants both simplicity and grandeur. But no words can describe the majesty of the interior. Its vastness is in some degree lost to the eye by the proportion which the height bears to the length, and indeed which all the parts have to each other. Some think this is a fault— for they say that the effect is thereby diminished, and perhaps they are right. I had fancied to myself a church darkened with something of the gloom with which we are familiar in the "dim religious light" of Gothic cathedrals, and which harmonizes so well with devotion. But in St. Peter's there is nothing of the kind. It is not only the largest, but the brightest, cleanest, lightest (if there is such a word) church in the world. There is no tawdry ornament, and nothing to distract the eye and interfere with the sense of its immensity, unless I except the colossal marble statues of apostles and saints in storm-tossed drapery, by Bernini—figures which are happily described by Dickens, in his "Letters from Italy," as "breezy maniacs." Nothing can exceed the richness and beauty of the marbles lavished in costly profusion everywhere in the interior, and the whole is kept with a degree of care and attention more like what might be expected in a drawing-room than in such a gigantic edifice.

As you go up the nave on the right hand, before you get up to the cupola, there is a very old bronze statue called St. Peter, the toe of which is devoutly kissed by every Roman Catholic who passes it. I saw the ceremony frequently performed, and with great fervour. There is some reason to believe that this statue is of pagan origin, and that it formerly did duty for Jupiter. I remember that at Pisa a statue was shown me in the cathedral by the sacristan which he said was an old statue of Mars, but it had been baptized, and it now stands as the figure of a saint. In the centre of the church, under the cupola, is a magnificent altar with a canopy over it called baldacchino below which is a crypt with steps leading down to it ; where, according to the tradition, repose the remains of St. Peter. And in the hollow space immediately in front of the door of the crypt at the foot of the stairs is a most beautiful statue of Pope Clement XVI. in the attitude of prayer, by Canova. There are also some magnificent pictures in mosaic, which look exactly like oil paintings, and are I suppose the finest specimens of the art in the world. Let us however leave the interior, and ascend to the top of the dome, where in the bronze ball above it, which looks from the ground not much bigger than a saucepan, there is in reality room for sixteen persons to stand. A special written permission must be obtained to make the ascent; and, armed with it, I mounted to the top, in company with two friends, during a tremendous thunder storm. This added very much to the sublimity of the effect, for the lightning flashed and the thunder pealed, and the rain rushed down in torrents, while a dense black cloud travelled from the west over the Campagna and hung like a funeral pall over Rome; until at last it cleared away, and we had a magnificent prospect in every direction except the north-east, where the sky still remained dark and sullen, and a fog obscured the view. One effect of our aërial elevation was the complete disappearance of the seven hills. They could not be distinguished by any difference of height

from the surrounding level—and this will perhaps
give you as correct a notion as you can have of
their really insignificant height. Looking south-
east, Rome lies spread out like a map before us,
with the Sabine and Latin mountains in the
distance, and on the west across the Campagna
are the blue waters of the Mediterranean, towards
which we see the yellow stream of the Tiber
winding its way.

Immediately below on the left is the Vatican,
and we see its form better here than from any
other point. We look down upon the private
garden of the Pope, and the quadrangles enclosed
by the long line of building which extends from
St. Peter's to the city wall.

As we ascend the upper part of the dome we
find that the stair winds between its outer and
inner wall, just as you might insert a knife
between the skin and pulp of an orange; and the
names of illustrious visitors who have mounted up
there are carefully recorded at full length on the
wall. Amongst others I remember those of Queen
Christina of Sweden, the Duke of Sussex, and
the late Emperor Nicholas of Russia. There are
two galleries, a lower and an upper one, which
run round the interior of the dome, into which
doors lead you from the staircase, and it is looking

down from these that we get an adequate idea of the immense elevation of the roof. One or two priests who were moving about below looked not much bigger than black rabbits. Some repairs of the mosaics in the cupola were going on while I was there, and I confess I admired the courage and nerve of the workmen who stood on the scaffolding at that tremendous height.

The art treasures of Rome are chiefly to be found in the Vatican and the Capitol. But besides these there are some most valuable collections of pictures in private palaces, such as those of the families of Borghese, Doria, Corsini, Colonna, and Barberini. In the Vatican there is a wilderness of ancient statuary and sculpture, and you wander from room to room, and from corridor to corridor, lost in admiring wonder. Here is the statue of the Apollo Belvidere, so beautiful that, when it was taken to Paris by the French at the beginning of the century, a young French girl by gazing on it went mad from love; and here also is the group of the Laocoon—the priest of Neptune, and his two sons, writhing in the twisted folds of two enormous serpents.

Amongst the pictures in the Vatican, the most celebrated are the Transfiguration, and Madonna di Foligno, by Raphael; and the Last Communion of St. Jerome, by Domenichino. I shall not venture to do more than pay my humble tribute of admiration to these glorious works. It would be presumptuous in me to attempt to criticise them, and I willingly leave to others the merit of discovering or repeating that in the Transfigura-tion proportion is not accurately kept—that Mount Tabor is not represented as high as it ought to be, and that the double action of the picture is an offence against the law of unity. This I know, that the effect upon the eye and mind of an ignorant beholder, like myself, is that of transcen-dent excellence; and I should, without hesitation, pronounce it the greatest painting I ever saw, were it not that I recollect the Assumption of the Virgin by Titian in Venice, which may well dispute the palm of pre-eminence.

But besides these oil paintings there are the frescoes of Raphael in the Stanze, and those of Michael Angelo in the Sistine Chapel. The Stanze are four rooms in the Vatican, decorated with frescoes by Raphael, and known each by a name taken from the principal subject on the walls. Thus the first is called the Stanza of the Incendio del Borgo, from the painting in it which represents the destruction by fire of the suburb at Rome called the Borgo in the ninth century, when it

was chiefly inhabited by Anglo-Saxon pilgrims.
The second is the Stanza of the School of Athens,
from the celebrated picture of the Greek philoso-
phers assembled together in a portico at Athens;
the idea of which has been lately reproduced in
an admirable fresco in the hall of Lincoln's Inn
by the living English painter Watts. The third
is the Stanza of Heliodorus, where the principal
fresco represents the Expulsion of Heliodorus
from the Temple ; the story of which you may
read in the book of Maccabees in the Apocrypha.
The fourth is the hall of Constantine, which
derives its name from the magnificent fresco of the
battle between the rival Emperors Constantine
and Maxentius not far from the Pons Milvius,
the modern Ponte Molle, to the north of Rome.
It was designed by Raphael, but executed by
Guilio Romano, and is the most wonderful battle-
piece in the world, whether we regard the immense size of the painting, the number of figures
introduced, or the action and spirit of the com-
position. This great battle decided the fate of the
Roman Empire, and it is well worth your while
to read in Gibbon the account of the events
that led to it, and also his spirited description of
the struggle. He says, after mentioning that Constantine, distinguished by the splendour of his

arms, had charged in person the cavalry of his rival, and that his irresistible attack determined the fortune of the day—

" The confusion then became general, and the dismayed troops of Maxentius pursued by an implacable enemy rushed by thousands into the deep and rapid stream of the Tiber. The Emperor (Maxentius) himself attempted to escape back into the city over the Milvian Bridge, but the crowds which pressed together through that narrow passage forced him into the river, where he was immediately drowned by the weight of his armour. His body, which had sunk very deep into the mud, was found with some difficulty the next day."

It is the moment of the rout the painter has seized on to represent in his picture, but Maxentius appears struggling in the water on horseback, not as having been pushed off the bridge by the crowd, but as having plunged into the Tiber to escape the vengeance of Constantine, who is close in pursuit.

The other great fresco in the Vatican is that of the Last Judgment, by Michael Angelo, in the Sistine Chapel. It occupies the whole of the side of the chapel that faces you at the end as you enter. It represents our Saviour, with the Virgin on His right hand; and a crowd of saints, and patriarchs, and martyrs on the right, while angels sound their trumpets and announce the Day of Doom. On their left are the damned, whom devils are seizing as they vainly struggle to escape, while Charon ferries a party across the Styx, and strikes down with his oar some of the refractory spirits. In one part of the picture is represented the Resurrection, and the blessed are seen rising from three graves assisted by angels. Michael Angelo was occupied with this work eight years, and it was first exhibited to the public on Christmas Day, 1541. When he was sixty-seven years of age, Paul III., who was the pope, gave him a life pension of 1,200 golden crowns, and his brief conferring this annuity says, " With apostolic authority, and by virtue of these presents, we concede to you during your life the pass of the Po at Vicenza." What this pass of the Po was I really am not able to say.

The roof of the Sistine Chapel is also decorated by frescoes from the hand of the same painter, representing scenes in the history of man from the Creation to the Deluge, with grand figures of prophets and sybils, in triangular compartments. at the sides of the ceiling. The best way of looking at them—and, indeed, the only way to see them properly—is to lie down flat on your back along

a bench and gaze upwards. It is said that Sir
Joshua Reynolds did this for so long a time, when
he was at Rome, that he never afterwards was
quite free from a pain in his back.

It would, however, be wholly impossible to
attempt a description here of the treasures of art,
which render the Vatican the richest museum in
the world. I must, therefore, pass over in silence
its long galleries of statues, and busts, and old
inscriptions, and Etruscan and Egyptian antiquities; and I will conclude with two of the most
celebrated statues at Rome which are not in the
Vatican, but in the Museum of the Capitol. I
mean the Dying Gladiator, and the Capitoline
Venus.

The name of the first is, however, a misnomer,
for it is not the figure of a gladiator at all, but of
a barbarian chieftain dying in the field of battle.
Most probably it represents a Celtic warrior, for
there is a ring round the neck, which was a
favourite mode of ornament, and T. Manlius
Torquatus derived his surname from slaying in
battle a gigantic Gaul and taking off from his
neck a chain (*torques*), which he placed round
his own. The unsheathed sword and broken
trumpet lying on the ground, with the gash in
the right side from which the life-blood flows,

proclaim the deadly nature of the combat in which he has sunk down to die, not, as Lord Byron describes him,

" Butchered to make a Roman holiday,"

in a gladiatorial show, but on the spot where he has fought with the Roman legions. The expression of the face is indescribable—the agony of approaching death is there seen contending with unconquerable resolution, and there is a look of hopeless sorrow in the face as if the stricken warrior felt that he died in vain.

The other statue that most arrested my attention in the Capitol is the Venus. It was discovered only a few years ago by accident in a walled-up chamber amongst some ruins on the Viminal Hill. It is kept in a small room, and the ceremony is always gone through of unlocking the doors, which might just as well be left open. To me it seemed the most beautiful model of the human form I had ever seen; and I thought it superior to its only rival the Venus de Medici at Florence, which is on a much smaller scale.

But it would be inconsistent with the object I have in view, and with the title of this little work, to pursue farther the subject of the art treasures of modern times in which Rome abounds. That subject is in itself almost inexhaustible, and no description can do justice to it. The pictures and statues must be seen to be appreciated. All that I wished to accomplish was to give an idea of the most prominent features of the Eternal City in connexion with her past history, and to point out the position of the ancient ruins as they now exist in their lonely desolation. They speak more eloquently than books can do of the departed grandeur and magnificence of the former mistress of the world. Time has thrown over them its funeral pall, and they stand like rocks on the sea, bare, silent, and melancholy; but no change of times or circumstances can deprive them of their charm I only wish I could hope by this slight sketch to communicate to others a small part of the interest with which the contemplation of them inspired me.

THE END.

LONDON : R. CLAY, SON, AND TAYLOR, PRINTERS.

Society

FOR

Promoting Christian Knowledge.

BOOKS SUITABLE FOR PRESENTS.

Most of these Works may be had in ornamental bindings, with gilt edges, at a small extra charge.

	Price.
	s. d.
ANIMAL CREATION, The. A Popular Introduction to Zoology. By T. RYMER JONES, Esq.	7 6
ASTRONOMY WITHOUT MATHEMATICS. By E. B. DENISON, LL.D., Q.C. Fcap. 8vo., cloth boards	2 0
AUSTRALIA ; its Physical Features, Inhabitants, Natural History, and Productions, &c. With a Map	3 6
BATTLE WORTH FIGHTING, The	2 0
BIBLE PICTURE BOOK, complete, containing 96 Plates, printed in three colors. Cloth boards.	5 0
In 2 Vols.:—OLD AND NEW TESTAMENT. Limp cloth *each*	2 0
BIBLE PICTURES and STORIES. In 2 Vols. With 96 Plates, printed in colors:—OLD AND NEW TESTAMENT. Extra cloth gilt *each*	7 0
BRITISH BIRDS in their HAUNTS. By the Rev. C. A. JOHNS	12 0
CARPENTER'S FAMILY, The. A Sketch of Village Life. By Mrs. JOSEPH LAMB (RUTH BUCK)	2 0
CHEMISTRY of CREATION	5 0
COLONIAL EMPIRE of GREAT BRITAIN, The. In Four Volumes. (Vol. I., 1s. 6d. ; Vols. II. to IV., each 2s.) Considered chiefly with reference to its Physical Geography and Industrial Productions. By the Rev. G. ROWE, M.A. Fcap. 8vo., cloth boards	2 0
DEWDROP and the MIST. By CHARLES TOMLINSON, Esq. New Edition.	3 6

(*Fcap. 8vo.*)

BOOKS SUITABLE FOR PRESENTS.

BOOKS SUITABLE FOR PRESENTS.

BOOKS SUITABLE FOR PRESENTS.

NEW COTTAGE WALL PRINTS. Printed in Colors, from Original Drawings by Eminent Artists. Size 14 by 11 inches. Hayfield, Cornfield, Strawyard, Trawling by Night, Storm, Bird's Nest. Each 6*d.*, in glazed frames 1*s.*, in gilt frames 2*s.*

DEPOSITORIES :

77, Great Queen Street, Lincoln's Inn Fields ; 4, Royal Exchange ; and 48, Piccadilly.